BLUE WILLOW

A NEWBERY HONOR BOOK

Also by
Doris Gates

THE WARRIOR GODDESS: ATHENA

LORD OF THE SKY: ZEUS

THE GOLDEN GOD: APOLLO

TWO QUEENS OF HEAVEN:
APHRODITE AND DEMETER

MIGHTIEST OF MORTALS: HERACLES

A FAIR WIND FOR TROY

A MORGAN FOR MELINDA

BLUE WILLOW

BY DORIS GATES

ILLUSTRATED BY PAUL LANTZ

VIKING · NEW YORK

TO MY
FATHER AND MOTHER

VIKING
Viking, a division of Penguin Books USA, Inc., 375 Hudson Street, New York, NY 10014
Penguin Books Ltd, 27 Wrights Lane, London W8 5TZ (Publishing & Editorial) and
Harmondsworth, Middlesex, England (Distribution & Warehouse)
Penguin Books Australia Ltd, Ringwood, Victoria, Australia
Penguin Books Canada Limited, 10 Alcorn Avenue, Toronto, Ontario, Canada M4V 3B2
Penguin Books (N.Z.) Ltd, 182–190 Wairau Road, Auckland 10, New Zealand

Copyright Doris Gates, 1940
Copyright © renewed by Doris Gates, 1968
All rights reserved
First published in 1940 by The Viking Press, Inc.
Published simultaneously in Canada
Printed in the United States of America by The Book Press, Brattleboro, Vermont
Set in Baskerville
Library of Congress catalog card number: 40-32435
ISBN 0-670-17557-9

30

CONTENTS

1. *THE SHACK*

JANEY LARKIN PAUSED ON THE TOP STEP OF THE SHACK AND looked down at her shadow. Just now it was a very short shadow even for a ten-year-old girl who wasn't nearly as tall as she should be. The squatty dark blotch running out from under Janey's feet didn't reach to the edge of the cracked boards. It was noon and the sun hung white and fierce almost directly overhead. It beat down upon Janey, the shack, and all the wide flat country stretching away for miles and miles in every direction. It was hot, so terribly hot that when Janey cupped her hands and blew into her sweaty palms her warm breath seemed cooler than the air she was breathing.

But it was better here on the steps than inside the stifling one-room shack where the heat of a wood-stove added its bit to the best that the sun could do. Besides, here you could look out across the shimmering heat waves to the west, where the mountains were supposed to be. And somewhere on the other side of the mountains was a blue ocean. At this season the heat hid the mountains, which were far off, anyway, and not even a breath from the ocean could find a way through the hidden ranges into this wide and scorching San Joaquin Valley. But earlier in the day, while they were driving here, Janey's father had told her there was an ocean to the west. So, lowering herself onto the top step, she sat humped and listless while she tried to find comfort in thinking about it. She looked very small and very lonely sitting there. Even her shadow, now she had seated herself, had shrunk almost to the vanishing point, abandoning her to the heat.

Across the road was another board shack a little larger and more substantial-looking than the one in which the Larkin family had found shelter. Already Janey had learned that a Mexican family named Romero lived there. Dad had gone over to talk with them soon after the Larkins had arrived here this morning. Janey wondered without much interest what their neighbors were like. Dad hadn't said whether there were any children or not. Of course there would be, though. Every family had children. Every family except the Larkins, that is. Sometimes, as now, Janey regretted her lack of brothers and sisters. Big families always seemed to have a better time of it than she did. Even when they were fighting.

Of course she might scrape acquaintance with the family across the road. Janey considered this possibility for a moment before she discarded it. No, it wouldn't be any use. She wouldn't be here long enough to make it worth her while. Besides, it was just as well not to get too thick with strangers. Saved you a lot of trouble.

"Takes two to make a quarrel," Mom always said. "Mind your own business and the other fellow won't have to mind it for you."

Mom was right, Janey supposed. Mom was nearly always right. Still there were times when this stand-offishness seemed vaguely wrong. It was at best a lonesome business. Right at this particular moment, for instance, she would have welcomed a quarrel as a pleasant break in the monotony of sitting here on the front step staring listlessly at a house across the road.

Suddenly her sagging shoulders straightened a little and an expectant look widened her blue eyes. A little girl with a baby in her arms had just come out of the Romero house and was now starting across the road toward the Larkin shack. For a moment Janey intently watched her approach and, when she was sure the girl and baby were really coming her way, she called a warning over her shoulder.

"Here comes one of the Romeros with a baby."

There was no answer from inside, only the sound of a garment being rubbed along a washboard. Mrs. Larkin was taking advantage of the present halt to do the washing. It wasn't a very big job, since the Larkins didn't possess a great quantity of clothes. But it takes a little time to rub out even one tubful, and this was the first real chance she had had to do it in many days.

With some surprise, Janey watched the Mexican girl pick her way amongst the greasewood and tumbleweed. It hadn't occurred to her that one of the Romeros might seek her out. When the stranger was within easy hailing distance, Janey called "Hello," with careful indifference. But her eyes were alert.

"Hello," came the answer, rather shyly given. The newcomer stopped in front of the steps as if she were awaiting judgment and shifted the baby in her arms.

"My name is Lupe Romero," she said. "This is Betty"—giving the baby another bounce. "She's kind of bashful, so I brought her over. It's good for her to see people."

Janey had expected the girl to offer an excuse for her visit. You didn't go out of your way to meet strangers without good reason. Betty seemed a satisfactory one.

"I'm Janey Larkin. Why don't you sit down?"

Lupe lowered herself onto the bottom step and deposited Betty beside her.

For a moment neither of them could think of anything to say, then, "It's sure hot, isn't it?" Lupe ventured.

"Yes," said Janey. "Awful hot."

"I saw you when you got here this morning," said Lupe. "I would have come over right away but my mother said to wait. How long are you going to stay?"

Janey was used to this question. She had answered it many

times in the past five years, and always she gave the same answer as she now gave to Lupe.

"As long as we can," said Janey.

"Did they say you could move in here?"

"No," Janey replied. "Dad said it didn't look as if anyone had been staying here for a long time, so we thought maybe it wouldn't matter if we did."

"My father says this house belongs to the man who owns that herd in the next field where the windmill is," Lupe explained. "No one has lived in this house for a long time."

"How long have you lived over there?" Janey nodded toward the house across the road.

"A little over a year."

Janey's cloak of indifference fell away from her.

"Have you been staying in that place for a whole year?" she asked in astonishment. It was a wonderful thing for a family to remain put for so long a time.

"Sure," said Lupe, making a grab for Betty, who had wiggled off the step. Then, "Where did you come from?" she asked when Betty was safe again.

"Do you mean in the beginning or just lately?" asked Janey. It made a difference in the length of the answer, for the whole story of the wanderings of the Larkin family since they had left northern Texas to come to California would have taken longer than Lupe might have cared to listen.

"I mean where did you stay last before you came here?"

"We camped down by Porterville last night. Dad came up here to work in the cotton."

"Have you any brothers or sisters?" Lupe asked pleasantly.

Janey shook her head and tried to look as if she didn't care.

"I have a brother"—Lupe's voice was smug—"and of course Betty. It is a good thing to have brothers and sisters," she added importantly. "It is too bad you have none." This last was in a tone of exaggerated regret.

Lupe was, of course, merely trying to make a teasing brother and a bothersome baby sound attractive. But Janey didn't know that and decided at once that Lupe was giving herself airs. Since it was a part of Janey's code never to feel inferior to anyone, something began to stir in her. Something that was a mixture of resentment and pride. She began to wonder if perhaps Lupe, though a stranger, already sensed her loneliness. Perhaps she was even feeling sorry for her. Well, she didn't need to! She would make that clear once and for all. Lifting her chin, Janey sent her words as from a great height to Lupe.

"I have a willow plate," she said. "A willow plate is better than brothers or sisters or anything."

Lupe's interest was caught on the instant. She was even impressed. But not in the way Janey had intended.

"You mean a plate made of willows? I have not heard of that before."

Janey gave her a pitying look, and felt much better for it. Lupe might have a brother and a sister. She might even have stayed in one house for a whole year. But she didn't even know what a willow plate looked like!

"Come inside," said Janey, tolerantly but with an eagerness that rather spoiled the effect. "I'll show it to you."

Lupe rose quickly, her dark eyes bright with curiosity. She picked up Betty and followed close on Janey's bare heels.

As they entered the house, a tall, thin woman with a tired face glanced up at them over a tub of steaming suds. The odor of soap and wet clothes in the stifling little room made the air seem too heavy to breathe.

"Mom, this is Lupe Romero, and her sister Betty."

Embarrassed, Lupe pressed her face against the baby in her arms.

"There's quite a family of you Romeros, isn't there?" Mrs. Larkin gave Lupe the ghost of a smile. "How old is the baby?"

"Six months," replied Lupe, answering the last question first, and daring to look at the grown-up. "I have a brother, but I'm the oldest. I'm ten."

"Janey's all the child we've got and she's a runty little thing. Skinny as a June shad." There were worry lines between her eyes as Mrs. Larkin studied Janey's blue-overalled figure. "It's moving about from pillar to post does it," she continued. " 'Tisn't any way to raise a young one, but a family's got to live somehow."

Janey acted as if she hadn't heard. She knew the words weren't really meant for her and Lupe, anyway. She knew Mom was just talking to herself as she did every now and then.

Lupe seemed to understand, too, and covered the awkward moment by looking curiously all about her. No detail of the room escaped her soft eyes.

The shack was not much to look at either for itself or for

its furnishings. The sides were rough, unfinished boards. Every crack and seam and knothole was there in plain view. It was exactly like the inside of a chicken coop, and not much larger.

In one corner was an iron bedstead with more rust than paint on it. The mattress, which spent most of its time traveling on the top of the Larkin car, had been dumped onto it along with a mixed heap of household things, including a roll of bedding. Across the room was a small stove as rusty as the bed. Two chairs placed facing each other were doing duty just now as a rest for the washtub. A wobbly table was the only other piece of furniture.

"You can hang these things over the fence pretty soon," Mrs. Larkin said to Janey. "I'll be needing another bucket of water, too." She wrung the last garment. "Help me dump this tub," she said, and Janey sprang to take hold of a handle.

Together they carried the tub to the back door and poured its contents out onto the parched ground.

"Do you want me to hang out the clothes right now, or can I show Lupe the plate first?" Janey asked.

"No, I'll save the last tub of suds for scrubbing up and I'll rinse after that. Then they'll be ready to hang out."

There would be plenty of time to show Lupe the plate, Janey decided thankfully. She needed a lot of time to show anyone the plate. Indeed, she never hurried in showing it to herself, for it was no ordinary plate. It meant to her what a doll might have meant if she had had one. Or brothers and sisters. And it meant much more, besides.

To begin with, it had belonged to Janey's great-great-grandmother, so it was very old. Then it had belonged to Janey's mother. But that was a long, long time ago before that mother had died and Mom had come to take her place. The memory of her mother was so shadowy to Janey that if she tried to hold it even for a second, it faded away altogether. It was like a bit of music you can hear within yourself, but which leaves you when you try to make it heard. Mixed up with this faint memory were Mother Goose rhymes and gay laughter and a home of their own. And because the willow plate had once been a part of all this, it had seemed actually to become these things to Janey. It was the hub of her universe, a solid rock in the midst of shifting sands.

In addition to everything else, the willow plate was the only beautiful thing the Larkins owned. It was a blue willow plate, and in its pattern of birds and willows and human figures it held a story that for Janey never grew old. Its color, deep and unchanging, brought to her the promise of blue skies even on the grayest days and of blue oceans even in an arid wasteland. She never grew tired of looking at it.

But, strangely enough, not once since the drought and dust storm had driven them out of Texas had the blue plate ever been used as a dish or for any other purpose. Never had it been unpacked except for brief moments. And never, Mrs. Larkin had declared long ago, would it be put out as a household ornament until they had a decent home in which to display it. In the meantime it was kept safely tucked away, a reminder of happier days before its owners had become wanderers in search of a livelihood.

Janey rummaged amongst the heap of things on the bed

and succeeded finally in hauling forth a scarred and battered suitcase. She worked it to one side of the roll of bedding, leaving a cleared space on the springs.

"You two sit there," she directed Lupe, who still held Betty in her arms. She tried to keep her voice matter-of-fact in spite of her growing excitement. She couldn't remember when she had ever been more eager to exhibit her treasure than on this occasion. Lupe would be dazzled. Never again would she boast of brothers and sisters in Janey's presence. Of course she couldn't be expected to appreciate the plate's whole significance. Nobody could except Janey herself. But no one could be indifferent to its great beauty. Not even Lupe Romero.

While Lupe and Betty made themselves as comfortable as possible on the wobbly bed springs, Janey opened the suitcase and carefully rolled back a top layer of folded things. Reaching in, she slowly lifted up the blue willow plate.

For an instant she held it at arm's length, her head tilted a little to one side so that the ends of her slightly wavy tow-colored hair bent against her shoulder. Then she drew the plate up level with her pointed chin and blew an imaginary speck of dust off it. Still holding it in her two hands, she placed it on the bed beside Lupe, and slowly let go of it. Not saying a word, she stood back, her eyes still feasting on the treasure, and something in her rapt face cast a silence over Lupe too.

As a matter of fact, so interested was Lupe in watching Janey's strange conduct that she didn't even so much as glance at the thing responsible for it. She was a little bothered by the way Janey was acting. Never outside of church had Lupe seen just such a look on anybody's face. It made her feel uneasy, and, clutching Betty to her, she at last slid her eyes toward the plate, half fearful of what she might see there.

But it was just a plate, after all, Lupe discovered. A pretty enough plate, to be sure, but certainly nothing to make such a fuss about. Its color she found distinctly disappointing. Why couldn't it have been red with a yellow pattern and perhaps a touch of green? But the gentle Lupe did not reveal her thoughts. Something in Janey's face forbade it. At the same time she was too disappointed to be able to say anything fitting. She had expected something marvelous and she had been shown what to her was a very ordinary plate.

Only to Janey did the willow plate seem perfect. Only for her did it have the power to make drab things beautiful and to a life of dreary emptiness bring a feeling of wonder and delight.

Bending over it now, she could feel the cool shade of willows, she could hear the tinkling of the little stream as it passed under the arched bridge, and all the quiet beauty of a Chinese garden was hers to enjoy. It was as if she had stepped inside the plate's blue borders into another world as real as her own and much more desirable.

For the moment she had quite forgotten Lupe, and it was only when a grimy finger descended upon the arched bridge and a small voice said doubtfully: "It's pretty," that Janey was jerked back to her real world of heat and soapsuds and poverty.

Lupe's questioning dark eyes were lifted to Janey's blue ones, as deeply blue now in their excitement as the plate itself. "But why does it have such funny-looking houses and people on it?" Lupe was trying to be polite.

"They all mean something," Janey explained. "You see, the plate has a story. Dad has told me about it lots of times." Then eagerly: "Would you like to hear it?"

Lupe nodded without much interest, but Janey didn't notice. Had Lupe been so cruel as to shout: "No!" it is more than likely that Janey would have insisted on telling the story anyway. It was nice, of course, that Lupe had nodded, but not absolutely necessary so far as Janey was concerned.

"Once upon a time over in China there was a rich man who had a beautiful daughter," she began.

"Were they Chinamen?" asked Lupe incredulously.

"Sure. They lived in China, didn't they?" Janey was annoyed at the interruption. She scowled at her listener, who looked apologetic and was silent as Janey went on.

"Well, this rich old man had promised another rich man to let him marry the beautiful daughter. But the daughter was already in love with a poor man who was very handsome. And when the father found it out, he shut his daughter up in a tower. See, here it is in the picture. But the handsome man stole her away, and they ran across the bridge to an island and there they lived for quite a while. But the father found out about it and went to the island to kill them."

At this point, Lupe furtively looked in the direction of Mrs. Larkin. But Mom wasn't listening to Janey's chatter. She was too busy with her own affairs.

Janey, noting that Lupe's interest had wavered for the moment, paused until her visitor's round dark eyes should be once more directed at the plate. Lupe misunderstood the pause and, eager to know the outcome, asked breathlessly: "Did he kill them?"

Janey ignored the question. This was the great moment in the story; she couldn't think of giving it away with a paltry "yes" or "no."

"He went to the island to kill them," she repeated, relishing the suspense, "and he would have done it, too, but just as he got to their house, something changed the lovers into two white birds, and so they escaped and lived happily ever after."

"What changed them?" asked Lupe as soon as Janey had finished.

"I don't know, but something did."

"It was a miracle," Lupe announced awesomely.

"I don't know much about miracles," Janey confessed. "But Mom says things just happen and you have to make the best of it, so I guess that's what the lovers did. Anyway, it would be sort of fun to be a bird," she added dreamily, bending over the plate.

"What kind of trees are those?" Lupe pointed to some waving, frond-like branches that swept almost across one side of the plate.

"Willows. That's why it's called a willow plate."

"I know what willows are; there's lots of them along the river, but they don't look anything like those on that dish," declared Lupe stoutly, defending her ignorance.

Janey chose not to argue the matter. "Whereabouts is the river?" she asked instead.

Lupe slid off the bed and took Betty into her arms again.

"Right over there," she said, balancing the baby on one hip in order to point from out the back door with her free arm.

Janey came and stood beside her in the doorway. Away to the east she could see a billowy line of foliage which distance had shrouded in a misty blue. It seemed to begin nowhere and to end in nothing. That was because one curve of the river swept it within her sight and another drew it away again.

"That's the river," Lupe informed her, adding with a wistful sigh: "I wish it was closer."

"How far away is it?" Janey asked.

"About a mile."

"We must have come by there this morning," said Janey, speaking more to herself than to Lupe. "It's nice to know there are willows here just as there are in the plate."

Lupe turned on Janey dark eyes in which there lay a mild hint of vexation. "But they aren't anything like those in the plate," she said reprovingly.

Janey didn't answer for a moment. A wise smile played at the corners of her mouth as she continued to gaze dreamily toward the river, indifferent to Lupe's troubled glances.

"From here they are exactly the same," she said at last, her voice almost a whisper. "They're even blue like the plate. Maybe there's a little arched bridge near them too."

Lupe's face brightened. "Yes," she said, relieved that Janey was beginning to talk sense, "there's a bridge where the high-way crosses the river, only it hasn't got any arch."

Janey looked at her with heavy scorn. "Can't you ever make believe about things?" she asked. "I don't mean an old highway bridge. I mean a little bridge with a house by it like there is in the plate."

Lupe shook her head slowly. "I don't know about that. Maybe there's a house there. I can ask my father."

"No, don't." Janey spoke quickly. "I'd rather not know if there isn't one. And if I don't know for sure, I can keep on playing there's one."

Lupe surveyed Janey with real interest. It was funny the way this strange girl talked almost as if she saw things other people couldn't see. Lupe wasn't altogether certain that it was safe to be too friendly with that kind of person. Maybe she was just queer and therefore to be avoided. But she didn't look queer, and it was sort of fun to hear her talk. You couldn't tell what she would say next. She sounded like some-body out of a story book or a movie. Lupe had never been around anyone like this before and she found the experience rather pleasantly exciting. In Janey, thoughtful now over something which Lupe was at a loss to understand, she could sense a difference that set this newcomer apart from all other people. Weighing the matter slowly and carefully, Lupe de-cided at last that she liked Janey in spite of her difference. On the heels of that decision came the hope that the Larkins wouldn't soon move away.

A tired voice behind them put an end to Lupe's thoughts and recalled Janey from her daydreams.

"You can hang these clothes out along the fence now, Janey."

Lupe hesitated for a moment, undecided what her position as visitor demanded in such a situation, then her natural courtesy came to the rescue. "I'd help you, Janey, only if I put Betty down, she'll start to cry."

"That's all right," said Janey, absently. Her eyes were still on the river.

Lupe edged out the back door. "Come over to my house when you get through," she said, adding: "The plate is real pretty, and I hope you stay here a long time."

Janey didn't reply immediately but continued to stand quietly gazing out the back door. Puzzled, Lupe began to move away, wondering if her polite little speech had been heard at all. At length, with a start, Janey became aware of her guest's departure and turned to Lupe like someone just awakened from sleep. The little Mexican girl with Betty in her arms had already covered half the distance to the corner of the house, the baby looking back owlishly over her sister's shoulder.

"Thanks, Lupe. I hope we stay here, too," Janey called to her just as Lupe rounded the corner and disappeared from sight.

Then Janey went over to the tub of clean clothes, picked it up, and started with it to the back door. But she didn't go directly outside. Instead, she halted in the doorway and stood there musing while the tub pulled her thin arms straight. At that very instant there had come over her the distinct feeling that something fine had happened. Not just the feeling she always had when looking at the willow plate that something fine was about to happen. This time it actually had. Lupe had said she hoped they would stay! It was the first time anyone had ever said that to Janey. A new warmth was encircling her heart, the kind of warmth that comes there only when one has found a friend. She stood perfectly still to let the full joy of the discovery travel all through her. It didn't really matter now that Lupe had thought the river willows different from those in the plate. Lupe had actually said she hoped they would stay! At that moment, Janey would have forgiven her anything.

She turned back into the room. "Lupe's nice, isn't she?" She sounded almost fearful. Everything depended on Mom's answer.

"She's a very well-mannered child," said Mrs. Larkin without enthusiasm.

But Janey was more than satisfied. She started away with the tub, a smile on her lips. While the Larkins remained in this place, Janey would have a friend. No longer would she have to feel lonely. There would be Lupe as well as the willow plate. And with that thought, Janey walked out into the blazing sunlight, her step as light as the washtub would permit.

2. "AS LONG AS WE CAN"

WHEN JANEY RETURNED FROM HANGING OUT THE WASHING, SHE found the boards of the cabin floor darkened with moisture and the smell of wet wood adding one more odor to those already filling the room. Mom was leaning a stubby broom against the wall.

"I couldn't do a proper job," she said, frowning down at the uneven boards, "the floor's too rough. But a broom and hot suds can do a lot with elbow grease mixed with them."

Janey looked at the floor without comment. It seemed all right to her, even if Mom wasn't satisfied. Why was she always fussing about dirt? Janey wondered, irritably. As a matter of fact, Mom fussed about a good many things. Lately nothing seemed to please her. The tired look hardly ever left her face. Of course Mom would be happier if they didn't have to move about from place to place. But there wasn't anything they could do about that. Dad had to look for work wherever work happened to be and it never lasted long in any one spot. Janey could feel herself beginning to lose patience with Mom, then remembered in time that Mom had liked Lupe. Besides, she undoubtedly meant all right and maybe it was better to prefer cleanliness to dirt, although it was a lot more trouble.

"I might as well stir up some corn dodgers as long as the oven's hot," Mrs. Larkin continued. While Janey watched, she wiped off the rickety table, produced a bowl and a small sack of yellow cornmeal and set to work. Janey eyed her speculatively. Would this be a good time for begging leave to return Lupe's call? She was nearly on the point of asking when Mom turned to her.

"As soon as I have this in the oven, we can start putting the place to rights. I can't seem to get used to living in a mess. Don't suppose I ever will, or I wouldn't mind it much by this time."

"I can untie the bedding and make up the bed," offered Janey in a small voice.

"No, it's too heavy for you. Wait till I'm through here."

Janey's neighborly inclinations strengthened.

Then, as if it were an afterthought, Mom said: "Have you done your reading yet today, Janey?"

"Not yet," admitted Janey. The two words seemed to put as many miles between herself and Lupe.

"Then you'd better be at it. You know what your father'd say if you let a day pass over your head without doing your stint."

Janey knew perfectly well what Dad would say if she neglected the two pages of Scripture which she was required to read daily. Dad believed there were some things second only to food and shelter in one's life. Reading was one of them.

So now Janey slid resignedly off her chair and dug to the bottom of the suitcase that held the willow plate. She lifted out a black leather-bound book, its back and edges worn.

It didn't seem strange to her that she should be using the Bible as a text book. It was almost the only text book Janey had ever known. Following the harvests from place to place had left her little time for schooling, even in the camp schools provided for the use of children like her. Sometimes, as now, she wished a little wistfully that she might some day go to a "regular" school where there were plenty of books, even new books, enough for every child. It occurred to her suddenly that probably Lupe went to such a school. She had lived here a whole year. Surely she belonged by this time. Janey walked slowly back to her chair, wondering what it would be like to belong. To go to school every day, a "regular" school, week after week, month after month.

She had seen a school like that once. It was over on the coast; she didn't remember just where. They had had to stop to change a tire right in front of the school house. It was a red brick school house, with white columns in front and a green lawn that stretched nearly to the road. Janey, feeling unusually daring that day, had crept up the walk until she could reach out and touch the smooth white columns. Glancing back at the car, she had made sure that her father and mother were still busy with the tire. And then she had edged along the building, her clothes brushing against the rough bricks until she was able to peep into a window. Inside was a room full of boys and girls. Some were sitting at desks, others were writing at the blackboard, and all of them looked as if they belonged. For a long time Janey stood there watching, until a shout from the car sent her speeding back along the way she had come. It is doubtful if any in the school room had known they were being spied upon.

Yes, it would be nice to go to such a school. She wished she were there now. It would be lots more fun than sitting here in a stifling room, poring over tiny print full of "thee's" and "thou's" and words her tongue stumbled over when she asked their meaning. Still, she had learned to read by this strange method, and she supposed it would be a very good thing to know how to read if she should suddenly find herself in a district school, though goodness only knew how that would ever come about. And then, besides that, there were undoubtedly good stories in the Bible. Very good stories indeed. Daniel in the lions' den, and Noah's Ark, for instance.

She decided she would read about the Ark and the Flood today. It was a good time to read about a rain that lasted forty days and forty nights. It might help as much as the blue plate to lift the weight of the heat.

Perching herself on the chair and hooking her bare heels over its rungs, she opened the worn, black book and began to read. Now and then she would put her fingers on a word to fasten it to the page until she had sounded it out. No matter how many times she read the chapter, those queer names always caused her to hesitate a little.

The oven door had slammed shut on the corn bread and Mrs. Larkin had gone outside for a breath of what might be considered cooler air before Janey came to the last verse.

While the earth remaineth, seedtime and harvest, and cold and heat, and summer and winter, and day and night shall not cease.

She closed the book and squeezed it between the two patches that covered her knees. Her hands stroked the soft leather in a thoughtful way. There was really nothing to be worried about, she decided, thinking of that last verse and of Mom's fussing. God had promised that there would always be harvests, so Dad would always have something to do. While the earth remaineth. And even the hot weather couldn't last forever. Winter would have to come along some day. And there was the blue plate. Now, if only Mom didn't look quite so sad, and if only she, Janey, could go to a "regular" school, the world wouldn't have much the matter with it, she thought. And as if to prove it, she heard Mom say just at that moment: "You can run over to Lupe's for a while if you want."

It was sundown before Mr. Larkin came home. The shack had been settled for hours, the bed made, the suitcase shoved out of sight underneath it, while corn dodgers reposed in state in the middle of the table.

Once again, Janey was sitting on the top step to greet her father as soon as he should come into sight. Away off on the western edge of the world, a red and angry sun was being swallowed up in its own heat waves. It was nearly gone now, and the faintest hint of a breeze was beginning to stir a single hair here and there on Janey's tousled towhead. If only the wind would really make up its mind to blow, to blow good and hard and send this dead hot air ahead of it out of the valley, or at least to some other part of it! she thought.

And then a battered car came into sight up the road, and Janey, with a cry over her shoulder, "It's Dad!" was off the step in a bound and down to the road. She trotted along beside the car as it bumped across the uneven ground to the house—the heat, Mom's tired face, and even Lupe forgotten in this moment's joy. Dad was home again!

"Hi, young one," Mr. Larkin called as he slowly eased himself from behind the wheel. "Shouldn't run like that on a hot day. Your face's as red as a cock's comb."

Janey smiled happily and pressed close to him as he reached into the car and lifted out some parcels.

"Here," he said, "take these in to your mother while I lift out the cushion on the back seat."

Janey took the bundles into the house and presently her father appeared with the cushion to the back seat gripped awkwardly in his arms.

"Where do you want this?" he asked.

"Doesn't matter now," his wife answered. "When Janey goes to bed we'll put it across one of the doors. It'll be cooler."

For this was to be Janey's bed tonight as it had been for many, many nights before this one. In fact, Janey wouldn't have known how to sleep on anything else. It was all the bed she knew, and she found it entirely satisfactory in every way. Of course, now that she was ten, her feet stuck out over the end of it a little, but the suitcase, shoved across the end, solved this difficulty.

"Will the job last very long, Dad?" Janey wanted to know.

"Can't say exactly. More than likely, though. We'll keep on irrigating for a while, and when picking starts I can't see any reason why I shouldn't get in on that too. You never come to the end of work in a cotton patch, Janey."

"What's the pay?" Mrs. Larkin asked.

"Two bits an hour, and I worked eight hours. How much is that, daughter? Quick now."

He whirled on Janey and stood grinning while she turned over in her mind this problem in mental arithmetic. She fastened her eyes on his as if she thought she could read the answer there. And just when the grin was broadening accusingly, "Two dollars!" shouted Janey, as quick as that.

"Correct," said her father, beaming. "That's a right pert child we're rearing under our roof."

"There are times when I'm glad it isn't our roof, like now," Mom returned, and walked heavily to the table where the parcels which held their supper lay alongside the corn dodgers.

"It isn't much to brag about and that's a fact," Mr. Larkin agreed, looking critically around him, "but it sure looks a sight better than it did this morning before you took it over."

Mom did smile at this, and Mr. Larkin, much encouraged, added in a teasing voice: "It must be awful to love to scrub as much as you do, Clara, and then never have a house worth scrubbing. Maybe it'll be different some day."

"Maybe," she returned briefly, the smile gone.

For a moment Mr. Larkin looked at her, his face suddenly sad and his shoulders drooping. Then he turned to Janey.

"Come on, young one. We'd better rustle up some more firewood before it gets dark."

Side by side, the two figures, one very tall, the other very short, both clad in faded blue overalls, moved slowly over the plain back of the shack. Each of them dragged a gunny-sack and into these they poked whatever pieces of grease-wood branches or roots they could find. When the sacks were filled, Mr. Larkin took one in either hand and dragged them up to the back door. Then he and Janey took the water pail and went with it to the windmill in the neighboring field. It was necessary to open a gate strung with barbed wire in order to enter the field.

There were cattle in that field, large, red beasts that jogged away awkwardly and stood staring at the strangers as they opened the gate.

Janey hesitated.

"These steers won't bother us any. Not like real range cattle," Dad said, and Janey, apparently reassured, walked boldly beside him. Secretly, however, she was still a little apprehensive and regarded the cattle with suspicion.

"Lupe Romero from across the road came over today," Janey said while they waited for the bucket to fill. "She says the house we're in belongs to the man who owns this windmill and these cattle."

"Yes, I know," returned Mr. Larkin. "Her father told me this morning when I went over there."

"Does he know we're living in his house?" queried Janey.

"As far as I know he doesn't."

They were on the way back to the shack now. Janey closed the gate, then ran to catch up with her father, who had gone on ahead with the brimming bucket.

"Suppose he won't let us stay when he finds out; what will we do then?" she asked, a strange fear all at once seizing her. Suppose they should have to go away tomorrow or next day? She might never see Lupe again!

Mr. Larkin stopped and looked over her head to the west and thought a moment before replying. Janey searched his face anxiously.

"He'd probably let us stay if we paid him something every month. I'd rather do that than move to the cotton camp. We'd have to pay rent there anyway, and we're better off by ourselves, Janey, even if we have to do without some things in order to stay that way."

Janey nodded her head in quick agreement.

"The Romeros have stayed in their house for a year. Do you think he'd let us stay that long?"

"If we paid up, he probably would."

Suddenly a strange tingling began to creep all over Janey, and her chest felt all at once too small for what was going on inside of it. Perhaps they wouldn't have to move on after a month or so! Perhaps Dad was going to stay put and she and

Lupe could become real friends. She might even go to school wherever Lupe did. A "regular" school, not just a camp school for roving children.

Before she could gather her wits for a proper reply, her father was speaking again. "We'll have to call a halt somewhere pretty soon, Janey. Mom isn't well, hasn't been for a long time. Maybe if she could stay long enough somewhere to get a real good rest, it would make a difference with her. It's hard to say, though."

"Then we'll stay as long as we can?" Janey asked.

"Yes, as long as we can."

Janey sighed and her bare toes dragged a little as she followed Dad to the house. It was the same old question and the same old answer. What wouldn't she give to be able to say just once: "We'll stay as long as we want to"!

When they got inside, they found supper ready for them. By moving the table over to the bed, there were seats enough for all three. After the dishes were washed, they sat on the front steps until bedtime. The little breeze had strengthened, and the moon was lighting earth and sky with a radiance that was like balm to eyes still smarting from too brilliant sunlight. From the top of a pole at the road's edge, a mockingbird dropped three notes as silvery as the moon's own light.

" 'While the earth remaineth, seedtime and harvest, and cold and heat, and summer and winter, and day and night shall not cease,' " Janey remembered thankfully.

Across the road a light twinkled in the Romero house.

"And there's Lupe as long as we do stay," thought Janey with equal gratitude.

3. COUNTY FAIR

THE LARKINS HAD BEEN LIVING A WEEK IN THE BOARD SHACK
when one day shortly after lunch Lupe Romero again came
across the road. It was not the first time she had been over
since that day Janey had shown her the willow plate. Janey
and Lupe had become good friends and had done much
visiting back and forth. Janey liked the happy-go-lucky
Romeros, especially Lupe and her mother. The Mexican family never seemed to worry about anything. Janey found them
a pleasant contrast to Mom's constant fussing. She didn't
even resent Lupe's giggles, for she had learned in this short
time that you didn't have to resent a friend's laughing at you.

So far, no one had demanded that the Larkins either move on or pay rent. Janey couldn't believe that this good luck would last very long, but she decided to try to make the most of it while it did last and not to worry about the future. Dad had already said that unless the rent was too high, they would pay it rather than to go into the cotton camp, and so a rather settled feeling had crept into the little household.

Watching Lupe's approach, Janey noticed that today she was walking quickly with a certain purpose about her. Something special was up.

"What's the matter?" Janey called from the front steps, her voice concerned.

"We're going to the fair and my mother says you can come too," Lupe yelled back.

"What fair?" Something special certainly *was* up.

"The big fair in Fresno. There's one every year. Today is the first day and children can get in free. Don't you want to go?"

Did she want to go? Janey wondered how Lupe could be so stupid! Certainly she wanted to go. Even if she wasn't quite sure what Lupe was talking about, it sounded tremendously thrilling, and besides it was all of twenty-five miles to Fresno. The trip alone would be something. And she had never been to a fair in her life, so that would be a real adventure. She felt like doing a handspring off the front porch, but all she said was: "I'll have to ask Mom first." No use getting worked up about it until you knew what was going to happen, she thought.

"Are you dead sure it won't cost anything?" queried Mrs.

Larkin when Janey had made her exciting announcement.

"That's what Lupe said."

Just then Lupe herself came into the room. "Honest, Mrs. Larkin, it's the truth. All of us kids are going and we sure couldn't if it wasn't free."

Mrs. Larkin eyed Janey doubtfully for several seconds before she could make up her mind. She had never let this small girl go so far away from her before, and it took her a little while to get used to the idea. In the meantime Janey danced first on one bare foot and then on the other. At last she grabbed the toes of one foot in her hand and squirmed for all the world like an impatient stork, but her anxious eyes never left her stepmother's face. Was Mom going to fuss about this, too? But finally, "All right," said Mrs. Larkin, "you can start getting cleaned up while I go over and see Mrs. Romero. I want to be right sure I have the straight of all this. And I want to know for certain when you'll be coming back."

Before Mom had had time to get to the front door, Janey was at the back reaching high above her head to the washtub hanging just outside the door. Lupe helped her balance it and together they got it safely down. Janey dragged it into the middle of the room and poured a tea kettle almost full of warm water into it, then dumped in what remained in the cold water bucket. For a moment she looked dubiously at the three inches covering the bottom of the tub, but decided at last that it would be enough.

Lupe, with native delicacy, sensing that Janey might prefer to bathe alone, edged toward the front door.

"You can come over to our place as soon as you're ready," she said. "We won't leave without you."

"Thanks," said Janey, unfastening an overall strap. Then, on a sudden impulse, she pattered across the room and put an arm around Lupe. "Thanks for remembering about me. It was kind," she said.

Lupe wriggled away from the embrace with an embarrassed giggle. "Oh, that's O.K. I wanted you."

Janey watched her go down the steps, half fearful of letting her get out of sight. Suppose the Romeros should change their minds about waiting! Suppose at the last minute they should forget all about her! Close to panic, she darted back into the room, whipped off her clothes, and hopped into the tub.

By the time Mrs. Larkin returned, Janey had finished her bath and was ready to step into clean clothes. There could be no question as to which dress she should wear, for she had just one and kept it for special occasions. And because such occasions were few and far between in Janey's life, the dress had lasted for quite some time. In fact it still remained almost the right length, for Janey had not done a lot of growing since the dress was new and when she slipped it over her head and straightened it around her waist, the skirt brushed her brown legs just above her knees.

"Sometimes it's a blessing you don't shoot up much," Mrs. Larkin commented, eying the skirt, "but just the same it isn't right. I declare it worries me to see you looking so spindling."

"I'm all right, Mom. I feel fine, especially today. Just because I'm not as fat as Lupe doesn't mean I'm sick."

Janey forced a grin in an effort to reassure Mom, who might develop notions and ban the excursion.

"I'm not saying you're sick," affirmed Mrs. Larkin, "but you're way undersize for your age and that isn't right."

Janey didn't answer but dug into a box in the corner and hauled forth a pair of canvas sneakers. She thrust her bare toes into them and drew up the lacings. A few swift motions, and the shoes were tied. She glanced out of the window. Yes, the Romero car was still standing before the house. Lupe was as good as her word. They were waiting.

Mrs. Larkin had been busy in another part of the shack, and now she crossed the room and held out a clean white handkerchief to Janey. There was something knotted in one corner of it.

"Here," she said, "you may need this. I tied a nickel in it. It's yours to spend any way you want to."

Wonderingly, Janey took the scrap of cloth and held it gingerly as if it might explode in her hand. It was the first time she had ever had any money of her very own. She hardly knew what to say.

"I'll be careful not to lose it," was all she could think of saying as she carefully tucked the handkerchief into a pocket of her dress. Half shyly, she raised her eyes to Mom's face. The tired look was gone and in its place pride and devotion were shining equally. In that instant Mom looked happy, almost gay. Janey wondered with surprise what could have caused the change. Was Mom so glad that a little girl happened to be going to the fair? She could think of no other reason and decided that must be it. And with the decision there came to mingle with her astonishment a feeling of shame for ever having noticed Mom's fussing.

Mrs. Larkin bent to kiss Janey good-by. "Whether you lose the nickel or spend it, it's yours," she repeated.

Janey returned Mom's kiss in silence and walked quietly out of the house. On the steps she paused an instant to stand on tiptoe, her face tilted up to the wide sky. She was on her way to a fair with five cents of her very own in her pocket! It was a lovely world. If only they wouldn't have to move right away and spoil everything. But she wouldn't think about that. They were here today and probably would be tomorrow. That was looking ahead far enough. With a splendid leap, she cleared the steps and raced across the road.

Manuel Romero had gone to his work that morning with a friend and had left the car for his wife. Unlike Janey's father, Manuel didn't work in the cotton fields, but instead was the organizer of a group of Mexicans who worked under contract in the vineyards, of which there were thousands of acres in the San Joaquin Valley. Many of them bordered on the cotton fields as well as on the grazing lands, for the soil varied considerably in quality and content and the crops accommodated themselves to it. Manuel Romero, long a resident of the country, knew the ranchers round about, and since over the years they had found him a reliable source of labor supply, he and his group of workers found plenty to do. While their pay was never enough to make them rich, it was enough to keep them happy, and a more contented and agreeable family than the Romeros it would have been hard to find.

At least that's what Janey thought when, in the seat of honor next to Mrs. Romero, who was driving, she at last started upon her way. The rest of the Romeros were on the back seat. Tony was doing a lot of hopping around, and from the subdued giggles and occasional thumps Janey guessed that he was not behaving too properly.

A quick glance over her shoulder gave her a view of Lupe vigorously shaking her head and frowning at somebody on the floor. But her eyes weren't frowning. They were brimming with mischief. Lupe had dressed up to honor the occasion. She was wearing a deep pink gingham stiff with starch and almost new. Janey thought it made Lupe's dark skin look darker than usual, but Lupe smoothed its folds with obvious pride, so Janey decided it didn't really matter. Her blue-black hair had been braided into two plaits and these in turn caught up by narrow white ribbons on either side of her head, the braids forming a loop just below her shoulders. Janey would have given a good deal to have had her tow hair as dark and lustrous as Lupe's.

The weather was still uncomfortably warm, and heat waves danced on the road before them. Off across the wastelands with their white patches of alkali accenting the dark clumps of greasewood, mirages shimmered and beckoned and to anyone who didn't know better offered tempting stretches of blue water. But Janey was far too wise to be deceived, and knew very well that when you got there you would find only more alkali and more greasewood.

Once she touched her pocket to make sure of the handkerchief's safety. It was still there, as she had known it would be. How should she spend her nickel? Could you buy many things for five cents?

Mrs. Romero broke in on her thoughts. "You are quiet, Janey," she said with mild reproach. "You shouldn't feel strange with us now. You must laugh and be glad because we have the whole afternoon to play."

Janey turned her head quickly and met Mrs. Romero's kind dark eyes. For an instant they smiled into hers then flashed back to the road.

"I *am* glad," said Janey, scrooching her toes up inside her sneakers. "You can't even begin to think how glad I am."

"That's better," said Mrs. Romero, looking straight ahead of her and nodding approvingly.

The idea of mentioning the nickel occurred to Janey, but she promptly set it aside. Mom wouldn't want her to appear to be bragging.

All at once, the unmistakable fragrance of fresh water filled Janey's nostrils. It was as welcome as a cool breeze and could mean only one thing. They must be near the river. Excitedly, she craned her neck to look out of the car and saw water running along the side of the road and widening out across the land to form a slough. Cat-tails grew about in great abundance, and mudhens paddled importantly in and out of them. Here and there red-winged blackbirds balanced on a leaning reed. Now they were almost at the river. Janey bent forward. Yes, there they were, the willows. And they looked just like those on the willow plate. Would Lupe notice? They were green, of course, at this close range and they grew more thickly than in the picture. But as they passed over the bridge, Janey, glancing upstream, could see the green, frond-like branches waving far out over the water.

Even in that hurried view, she was touched by the charm of this place. Somehow she must contrive a way to make Dad bring her here. She felt the need of touching those willows, of dabbling her feet in that cool water. Perhaps Mom would come, too. They could bring a little food with them and stay all day. She wondered when that would be. Tomorrow? The next day? But they might be leaving tomorrow. Janey pushed that thought aside before it could have time to make her sad. This was not the moment to be downhearted. She was on her way to the fair! Tomorrow, with whatever it might bring, would have to wait until—tomorrow.

Long before they were able to see the fence enclosing the fairgrounds, Janey knew they were almost there by the way the traffic began to thicken. Mrs. Romero had to drive very carefully because of the boys and girls trooping along the side of the road in excited indifference to the line of cars moving with them. Janey eyed the children with some relief. Surely not so many would be going if it weren't free!

Just the same, she felt much better when at last, with the car safely parked, she walked in under the arch which marked the entrance and found herself actually at the fair and with her five-cent piece safe in her pocket. A double row of elms led from the entrance to the first building some little distance away, and as they strolled along Janey had a chance to get her bearings.

"Over there's the Ferris wheel," Lupe explained. "It's always in the same place."

"What's that fence for?" Janey pointed to the left.

"That's the race track, only they don't have races the first day." Lupe, having attended the fair every year since she was old enough to toddle, was thoroughly enjoying this chance to show her knowledge. It wasn't often Janey gave her such an opportunity.

But Janey didn't begrudge Lupe her small triumph. It was convenient to have someone at hand who knew all about it, and reassuring too. The crowd was increasing every minute and so was Janey's bewilderment. Only the stanch presence of the Romeros prevented her from being afraid of this strangeness all about her.

At mention of the race track, "Let's look at the horses first," begged Lupe's brother, so Mrs. Romero picked up Betty and they all started to the end of the fairgrounds where the livestock was housed. Janey had never seen so many animals gathered together in one spot. Sheep, hogs, horses, mules, and cattle were present in profusion, and all so clean and cared for they looked as if they had just come out of the Ark dressed in their Sunday best. Looking at them, Janey thought how nice it would be if people could, like the horses, grow glossy coverings that never wore out and which you never could outgrow.

In and out and around they sauntered until at length they found themselves in another building where there were exhibits of various kinds, patchwork quilts and jars of fruit as well as booths full of all kinds of fresh vegetables very elaborately arranged with the name of the town from which they had come prominently displayed amongst them.

"There'll be a prize given to the place that has the best display," said Lupe.

Great mounds of fruit rose temptingly higher than their heads. Oranges, apples, grapes, and pears. And everything was shining and luscious.

Janey was lost in admiration of this abundance. Nowhere except in the pages of the Old Testament had she ever come upon such bounty. She felt as the men sent to spy out the Land of Canaan must have felt. Surely this San Joaquin Valley was a land flowing with milk and honey! If she had ever stopped to think about it, she wouldn't have supposed there could be so many different kinds of things to eat in all the world, and here they were spread out before her feasting eyes, within reach of her hand.

This fruit simply begged to be eaten, she thought. It didn't want to sit here uselessly gathering dust and growing overripe. Suppose she should put out her hand right now and seize that particularly tempting pear? Would its absence in the midst of so many be noticed? Yes, she was forced to admit to herself, it would. There would be a gaping hole in the neat and orderly display. Besides, to remove a pear from this booth would be stealing, and Janey remembered in time that she was no thief. Resolutely, she turned her back on the fruit, only permitting herself one wistful sigh.

Mrs. Romero heard it. "Tired?" she asked anxiously.

"No," grinned Janey. "Just tempted. Let's get out of here before I start grabbing things."

In the next building were commercial exhibits. There was even a small stage where, at regular intervals, a magician did

tricks of amazing sorts, making handkerchiefs float out of
cans of oil, after which he poured oil from the cans, although
the handkerchiefs had been dry and clean. It was very wonderful and mystifying to Lupe and Janey in spite of Tony's
repeated assurances that anybody could do "a little old trick
like that."

The show over, they strolled on to the booth across the
way, and then Janey stopped suddenly. Before her she saw
what looked like a very comfortable living-room. There was
a rug on the floor, and tall lamps beside each chair.

She was puzzled. Could there be someone living in this
booth at the fair? But there was one thing strange about it,
that made it different from a real living-room. In its center
was a round table literally heaped with books. Big books
and little books, all of them shiny and new, had been arranged on some kind of rack so that from the table's edge
they rose in a circle to make a small mountain of books. And
it took only half a glance to see that they were books for boys
and girls. The gay covers caught Janey's eye and held her
spellbound. She felt drawn to that table as by some force
beyond her power to withstand. She couldn't have walked
past if she had wanted to. And she didn't want to.

"That's the liberry booth," said Lupe as casually as she had
indicated the Ferris wheel. "Just books."

Just books. Now Janey's curiosity was at its very peak. So
these were new books. The kind she might even handle
every day if she went to a "regular" school. Janey had never
had a new book in her hand. Now temptation was too strong
to resist. That invisible force was moving her toward the

table. Cautiously she advanced until she stood inside the booth. She looked about and felt stirring deep inside of her an old lost memory. Somewhere, sometime, she had seen a room something like this. A room in a house. But it had been long, long ago.

She approached the table and as she did so a woman appeared from around it.

"Come in and rest a minute," she said, just as if she had known Janey all her life. "These books are here for you to look at as long as you care to."

Reassured, Janey circled the table on tiptoe, forgetting all about the Romeros standing patiently outside. But Tony's patience was beginning to wear thin.

"Come on," he called. "We're going to the merry-go-round."

Janey quickly tore herself away from the books and walked straight up to Mrs. Romero. "I'd like to stay here a while," she announced firmly. "You all just go ahead anywhere you want to, and I'll stay here until you come back."

"Don't you want to ride on the merry-go-round?" asked Lupe, as if she couldn't believe her ears.

Janey shook her head. "I'd rather stay here than go anywhere else, I promise."

"Well," began Mrs. Romero, doubtfully, while Janey's eyes grew deeply blue in earnest appeal, "well, you be sure then that you don't start off anywhere until we get back."

"I promise you faithfully, Mrs. Romero, cross my heart and hope to die," and Janey went through the pantomime, looking as if she might expire instantly if permission were withheld.

So the Romeros moved off, a little uncertainly. Lupe looked back at Janey with perplexed brown eyes. She still was unable to accept the fact that Janey would rather pore over books than ride on the merry-go-round, and in Lupe's kindly heart a certain suspicion began to form. Perhaps Janey didn't have a nickel for a ride! A great sadness descended upon her, completely snuffing out the high carnival spirit which had possessed her such a short time ago. Then her dark little face set suddenly in lines of stubborn determination. Janey should have her ride; she, Lupe, would see to that; and the closer they came to the familiar and enchanting strains of the merry-go-round music, the more determined Lupe grew.

In the meantime, Janey, blissfully unaware of Lupe's troubled heart, was reveling in her new-found treasure. She hardly knew where to start. Each book was as inviting as the one next to it, but she could hardly read them all at once! She circled the table on tiptoe a couple of times, thankful that the woman, having invited her in, went about her own business, leaving Janey entirely to herself. She didn't want anyone to offer suggestions or to ask questions. All she wanted was to be let alone for as long a time as possible to enjoy the feast. At last she decided on her book, and picking it up as reverently as she always did the willow plate, she backed over to a chair and began to read.

She had been there perhaps fifteen minutes when all at once she felt Lupe's hand squeezing her shoulder and Lupe's voice saying into her ear: "I won the brass ring. It's good for a free ride, and I want you to have it."

It took Janey fully thirty seconds to understand what Lupe

meant, but when she did, her face flushed a bright crimson and her eyes flashed as cold as blue ice.

"Thank you," said Janey, minding her manners in spite of her humiliation, "but I don't want it. It's your ride, and besides I have my own nickel. I don't need to be beholden to anyone."

Lupe stared, aghast. This was not at all what she had expected. This Janey, always so touchy. She, Lupe, had hurt her friend's feelings and she had only meant to be kind. What could she do to make things right again? It was hard for the little Mexican girl to understand why Janey was angry with her. If you had things you shared them with your friends. Or so Lupe had always believed. And your friends accepted from you as a matter of course. For some reason, Janey didn't want to accept. Very well, then Lupe would fix it in such a way that Janey would not feel as if she were accepting anything. She would be doing Lupe a favor by taking the ring.

Slyly Lupe lowered her eyelids so that Janey might not detect her kindly falsehood.

"I know," she said quietly, "but I've been riding so much another would make me dizzy. That's why I thought I'd give the ride to you."

For a moment Janey studied Lupe's downcast eyes, while the ice slowly melted in her own. Roaming about the country into all sorts of places with all sorts of people had rendered Janey wise beyond her years, and now a sixth sense warned her that what Lupe had just said was not true. At the same time, one searching look into Lupe's eyes, now raised to hers and a little misty, made Janey equally certain that the offer had been proffered not out of pity but out of friendship. And something told her you could accept from a friend. Perhaps there were times when you had to. This was undoubtedly one of them.

She reached out her hand, and Lupe laid the brass ring on it.

"All right," said Janey, carefully keeping her eyes away from Lupe's face, "as long as you're sure you don't want it, I'll take it."

"No, I don't want it, Janey. It's O.K.," said Lupe softly.

So Janey had her ride on the merry-go-round, and after that it was time to go home. But first Janey must spend her five-cent piece. What should she buy? The Romeros were full of suggestions. Mrs. Romero advised an ice cream cone, and Janey's mouth watered. Tony thought a serpent balloon just the thing. They were standing before a little handcart at the side of the road beneath the elms, and it was hung with every imaginable kind of candy and cheap gimcrack.

"I know," said Janey at last, sounding very sure of herself. "It's just the thing, too." She stepped up to the cart and asked the man for a package of gum. While he reached for it, she finally managed, after some tugging, to free the nickel from the handkerchief and passed it over in exchange for the gum. Hastily she unwrapped the small package and offered a stick each to the Romeros with the exception of Betty, who was, of course, too young. That left one piece each for Dad and Mom. Then, with head held high, Janey walked along with the Romeros under the towering trees and through the gate, and away from the fairgrounds. It had been a good day!

4. JANEY WALKS INTO A PICTURE

BUT THE NEXT DAY WASN'T SUCH A SATISFACTORY ONE. THAT IS, in some ways it wasn't. Mom would have said it all depended on how you looked at it. Anyway, whether for good or for bad, the next day the Larkins were asked to pay rent.

Hardly had Mr. Larkin returned from work when a truck drove past the house and up to the gate leading into the field where the windmill was. A man got out of the truck, opened the gate, and went on into the field. He remained there for a short time, inspecting the windmill and looking over the herd. Returning to the truck, he seemed about to drive away, but instead pulled up beside the house and stopped. Without bothering to turn off the motor, he jumped down from the truck and bounded up the front steps of the shack.

"Hello, buddy," he called jauntily as Mr. Larkin rose and started toward the open door. "When did you move in?"

It was still broad daylight and Janey had plenty of opportunity to study their visitor. And what she saw she did not like. She couldn't decide exactly what there was about him to make her feel distrust. "It must be his eyes," she concluded. They moved shiftily about, never seeming able to rivet themselves on any one thing for more than a second. Moreover, his attitude seemed to indicate plainly that he held the destiny of the Larkins in the hollow of his very dirty right hand. The manner with which he stalked boldly into the house and looked casually about couldn't have made it any plainer. Janey had the feeling, even, that if there were anything in sight which he considered worthy of his interest it would become his on the spot. For once, she was extremely thankful that the blue willow plate was safely out of sight.

"Something I can do for you?" Janey could tell that Dad was indignant. His voice was hard and even. Evidently he felt exactly as she did toward this intruder.

"I'll say there is," returned the stranger. "You can just hand over five dollars a month rent for this shack. Rent starting from the day you moved in, whenever that was."

"We've been here a week," said Mr. Larkin.

The man narrowed his eyes for an instant while he thought rapidly. "Yeh," he finally said, "I guess that's about right. The last time I was out this way, there wasn't nobody here."

Mr. Larkin, ignoring this remark, walked away to speak in low tones. to his wife, who had remained at the stove, her back to the room. Now he faced the man again and said, reaching into his pocket and drawing forth a buckskin bag:

"Here's your money, and I'll take a receipt."

For just a second the man hesitated, then, "That ain't necessary, buddy. I'm Bounce Reyburn, everybody knows me around here."

"Just the same," said Mr. Larkin quietly, but drawing up the strings of the buckskin bag, "I'll take a receipt from you, or you won't take any money from me."

An ugly light came into Bounce's eyes, and Janey, catching it, felt a queer little shiver run along her spine. The glint remained for the merest instant and then Bounce shrugged and grinned, a little too broadly, Janey thought.

"O.K.," he said, "give me a scrap of paper, somebody, and I'll put my John Henry on it."

Janey produced some wrapping paper on which her father wrote the date and what the money had been paid for. Then he slid it across the table to Bounce, who scrawled his signature on it and flung it back.

"Do you own this place?" asked Mr. Larkin, folding the scrap of paper and slipping it into the buckskin bag.

"No, but I've got a stake in it." Bounce was moving toward the door. "I'm Anderson's foreman and he owns all this land from here to the river. But what I say goes," he added emphatically, shoving his hands into his back pockets and fixing Mr. Larkin with an insolent stare, "so don't you be runnin' to him and squawkin'. It won't get you nowhere."

Janey's father chose not to reply to this, and Bounce backed toward the door. "Well, be seein' you around," he said with a vague salute. "So long."

Janey watched him silently as he got into the truck and drove noisily away. Well, he was gone and with him five dollars of Dad's hard-earned money. But he hadn't said anything about their moving on. She didn't regret the money as she hugged this thought to her. Later that night, while she lay on the back seat cushion watching the stars winking at her as if she and the vast heavens shared a secret, Janey decided it was a relief to have the rent business settled once and for all. It was hard, of course, to see five dollars go from them when there was so much they needed, but it was good to know they would not have to move to the cotton camp. Probably this Bounce Reyburn would let them stay as long as they paid rent. Suppose they never had to move again! Suppose Dad could find work right here that would last forever! On this pleasant thought, Janey drifted into happy dreams.

The next morning, however, her peace of mind received a rude shock. Some time around nine o'clock, Mr. Larkin unexpectedly walked into the shack, announcing that there would be no work for the next three days. Something about the irrigating made a lay-off necessary. Janey felt sick with dread. The words "no work" always meant a move to another place. It was terrible to hear them spoken now, just when she was beginning to feel secure. Her face was such a picture of woe that Dad, catching sight of it, burst out laughing.

"Don't look so gloomy, young one," he said teasingly.

"There'll be more work in three or four days. So we won't be moving yet a while."

Janey was too relieved at his words to wonder how he could have read her thoughts so accurately. She could feel elation rising like a swift tide within her, erasing her woebegone look and lifting her on tiptoe.

Now the day seemed suddenly special, different from all other days. Dad was home, but there would be more work. They wouldn't have to move on yet a while. Therefore, this day mustn't be spent like just any day, she decided. It must be set apart and remembered. She brushed her hair out of her face with an impatient hand and scowled in concentration. What special thing could they do? She must think fast or Mom would be suggesting something for Dad to do and spoil everything. Something dull, but so necessary he would feel bound to do it. Like rustling stove wood.

All at once, her brow cleared and a light danced in her eyes. She was seeing what no one else in that room could see. Leaning willows and running water. Blackbirds balancing precariously on slender reeds. The river. That's what the day needed. And with the realization, that rising tide within her reached the breaking point.

"Let's go to the river," cried Janey in a voice as softly modulated as the screech of a peacock.

Mom whirled on her with a frown of irritation. "I declare, Janey, if you don't stop yelling your head off around here I'm going to take you in hand. It's wonderful to me how such a big sound can come out of such a small body."

"Yes, ma'am," said Janey meekly, subsiding into a corner.

But her face was as eager as that of a terrier who is forced to sit idly by while the visiting dog gnaws his bone. Should she repeat what she had just said? Was Mom really angry or only fussing? What was she doing with that frying pan? Now she was cutting off a slice of salt pork! Would Dad ever speak up? All at once a suspicion began to form in her mind. Why, Dad was just teasing her with his silence! She darted toward him.

"You *are* going to the river, aren't you?" she cried, and this time Mom only smiled, although Janey's voice had been as shrill as before.

"You bet we're going," said Dad at last. "That river ought to have some cats in it, and we'll catch a few or my name isn't Jim Larkin."

Now some people might have wondered just what Dad could be talking about, because anyone knows that cats and rivers don't go together. At least not as a usual thing. But Janey knew what Dad meant. He was talking about catfish, and catfish are very, very good to eat when they are fried crisp and brown right out of a river. Mom knew what Dad meant, too. She had even known what he was thinking. That's why she now had the frying pan and salt pork already tucked neatly into a paper bag.

Dad got out his fishing lines and they were ready to go. They decided to walk, as it was less than a mile to the river and they needed to be saving of gasoline. Three abreast, with Janey in the middle, they set out. The sun was hot; the sandy soil under their feet was hot. But Janey didn't notice. Her eyes were fixed on the ragged line of blue-green foliage that marked the river. There the willows grew, and in amongst them would be shade and running water and an endless number of delights that Janey couldn't have listed at the moment but which she could very plainly feel in her bones. It was the same feeling she always had when looking at the willow plate. Something fine was about to happen. Perhaps they would catch a lot of fish!

For a short distance from the shack, a few cattle stopped their grazing to amble along the barbed-wire fence beside the three. Janey, noting their sleek red sides, wondered how they could manage to get fat and stay that way on the dried burr clover, alfilaria, and squirrel grass they munched in such a satisfied manner. The matted plants grew close to the sandy ground as if they had wearied of trying to put forth stalks in this frugal soil. But the cattle seemed to like it, even if Janey didn't think much of it.

It was curious, too, she thought, that the country should be so spotty. On one hand was grazing land, on the other only bleak white sand against which occasional clumps of greasewood showed darkly. She questioned her father.

"That's because of the alkali," he answered. "Some places there's more of it than others, and wherever there's a lot of it, the plants can't grow. Except greasewood; nothing seems to bother that. The whole valley is spotty," he continued. "Some of it's rich and fertile, some of it's alkali and worthless. Some of it's in between and that's the stuff the sugar beets grow on, if water can be got to it. But cotton needs good soil. Cotton wants only the best."

"Except people," Mrs. Larkin put in. "It doesn't seem to

matter what sort of people work in the cotton, as long as there's plenty of them."

"Why, Mom, there never was a better man ever worked anywhere than Dad," said Janey stanchly.

Mom reached out a hand and gave her a little squeeze on the back of her neck. "That's the truth," she said quietly.

Dad didn't say anything, but he looked pleased.

Just then a jack rabbit popped out from behind a clump of greasewood and went bounding stiffly away.

"Now if we could only go as fast as that," said Janey looking wistfully ahead through the heat waves at the tantalizing line of the river.

They skirted the slough and little by little, step by step, the willows drew closer until finally the three stood beneath their grateful shade with the cool water gliding gently past.

It was all so lovely no one could think of anything to say for a moment. Then Mom broke the silence.

" 'Rivers of water in a dry place,' " she quoted, and Janey thought the words exactly right.

They sounded deep and quiet like the river itself. Hearing them, this spot, already so beautiful, seemed to take on an added beauty. Janey repeated them to herself, her lips moving softly over the words, and felt more grateful toward Mom than she had felt the other day on receiving the nickel; much more grateful because the money was already gone while "rivers of water in a dry place" would be hers forever. It would be something to hold to, like the willow plate.

At first Janey was content just to sit upon the bank, her toes curled into the cold mud while she listened to the quiet.

Tipping back her head, she could see, through the tracery of green, the pale sky above her. Just now a hawk was wheeling in it like a small lost shadow searching for its object. She looked around for Dad and saw him at a little distance intently studying the willow branches. At length he came up to her, a long switch in his hand.

"Here's your fish pole, Janey. See if you can get a catfish before I do."

"How can I catch a fish when I haven't any line or any bait or anything?" asked Janey, scrambling to her feet and dashing up to him.

"Hold your horses," he said with a laugh. "I'll soon fix that up."

And he did. Almost before she knew it, Janey was curled among the roots of an old willow, holding her pole straight before her and watching with eager eyes the particular spot where she hoped a catfish might be lurking. But of course nothing happened for quite a long time, and she was beginning to wonder where the hawk had gone and to crane her neck in search of him when all at once there was a sharp tug at the end of her line. Janey didn't squeal or do anything foolish. She had gone fishing many times before. She merely gave the line a little jerk to make sure that whatever was on it was firmly hooked and then she began to back up the bank. The catfish, for it was a catfish and a pretty good-sized one too, didn't put up much of a fight and in no time at all she had him out of the water and out of his gasping misery. Janey had caught the first fish!

Mr. Larkin caught the next two and then declared that the

sun was getting too high for fishing, even catfishing, so they leaned their poles against a tree and cleaned the fish in the river. Dad skinned them and Janey did all the rest, and she made a good job of it.

After that, it was Mrs. Larkin's turn. From the paper sack she drew out the skillet and put the salt pork into it. Janey's father built a small fire, the skillet was placed over it, and soon the catfish were sizzling in a way to make a hungry person hungrier than ever. When at last they were golden and crisp, and Mom pronounced them ready for eating, Janey couldn't wait for them to cool but scorched her fingers in her greediness to get at them.

"Serves you right," said Mrs. Larkin calmly, as Janey juggled the six inches of hot fish from one hand to the other.

"I know," said Janey, "but I'm *that* hungry."

The three sat in a close circle under the trees, and ate in silence. When the last scrap of fish had been eaten, Janey tucked the little handful of fish bones out of sight under the willow roots while Dad and Mom stretched out full length on the grassy bank.

"Now what more could a body want than this?" Mr. Larkin asked of no one in particular. "We've enough food in our stomachs, a little money in our purse, and a roof to go home to. I don't know when I've liked a place as well as this one."

Janey had been tracing patterns in the moist earth. But at Dad's words she stiffened with attention, listening with her heart as well as with her ears. Was he going to say they would stay? She hardly dared think so, yet why was he talking like this? He never had before, at least not within her hearing. Not even that night by the windmill had he sounded like this. There was a silence during which Mr. Larkin smiled vaguely into space. Janey sank back on her heels, pressing her palms tight against her thighs. She knew Dad was waiting for Mom to say something, but Mom didn't. She lay quietly with her eyes closed and a tired droop to her mouth. At last Janey could stand it no longer.

"Do you think, Dad, that maybe we might stay?"

"Why, I reckon we will, daughter. As long as there's any work, that is."

"But how long will there be work?"

"Can't ever say for sure. Maybe a month, maybe two. You can't ever tell."

Janey crept away and settled down again, cross-legged, her back to her father. No use letting him see how bitterly disappointed she was. For a moment her hopes had foolishly soared. She should have known better.

Her eyes rested upon the moving water, but she didn't really see it. Her thoughts were turned inward on herself. It was queer, she was thinking, how a girl named Lupe, and a county fair, and now this river could so change anyone as they had changed her. Only a short time ago, she would have taken whatever the day offered and been content with it. But now everything was different. Now she wanted to stay. Never again would she be quite the same Janey. Never again would she be entirely happy or content moving from place to place. Now she wanted to stay.

For fully five minutes she sat there while her heart gradually moderated its beat and her disappointment gave way to a feeling of resignation. No use spoiling this day by being downhearted and miserable over something she couldn't help, she decided. She glanced over her shoulder at Dad and Mom. They were asleep. Slowly, she got to her feet and began walking downstream, slipping along beneath the willows like a small blue ghost.

Ahead of her, the stream curved, beckoning her on. Perhaps if she followed around it, she would find a bridge and then she could explore the other side. Of course there was a bridge at the highway, but that was away off on the other side of the slough and so it didn't count. Now she had reached the bend, and rounding it she found just what she had hoped to find. There was a bridge, an old wooden one, and climbing up from the water's edge Janey came to the dusty little road which connected with it and went meandering off half-heartedly to the north. Neither the bridge nor the road looked as if it had been used a great deal. Janey walked to the middle of the bridge and stopped there to look back along the way she had come.

The river flowed deep and smooth and almost noiseless. Not a ripple disturbed its shining surface. It was more like a huge ditch than a river, she thought, and wished that the water weren't quite so deep. There was something exciting and at the same time friendly in the sound of a river tearing over a rocky bed. It was as if it were trying to tell you something. But this river was not like that. It seemed to hold a secret within its quiet depths, and Janey easily convinced herself that it was a good secret. Surely, she thought, no river that would bring its cool waters and its willows into such a hot and thirsty country as this could have any but the best secrets. Even if it was silent and mysterious, she loved it. And no matter where she might find herself in days to come, she knew she would never forget this San Joaquin River and this moment when she stood on a bridge above it. She couldn't have told anyone why she felt this way. She didn't try to understand it. It was enough that she knew.

Driven by the beating sunlight as well as urged on by her own curiosity, Janey crossed the bridge at last, her bare feet silent on the dusty planks. She followed the faint tracing of the road around a clump of willows and halted abruptly.

To her surprise, she discovered she had walked straight into somebody's dooryard. It was a very large dooryard, with three great willows as big as oak trees shading it. Off to one side was a low and rambling ranch house. Its weatherbeaten white paint and sagging green shutters showed plainly that it had been there for a long time. Off across the wide yard, at quite a distance from the house, a large barn sprawled lazily in the shade of a sycamore tree. There was no one in sight, and except for the droning of the cicadas not a sound broke the heavy midday quiet. Janey felt as if she had walked into a picture, but a picture that was strangely familiar. What made her feel as if she had been here before? Everything was as still as the castle of the Sleeping Beauty. But evidently her presence was all that was needed to break the magic spell. For in the next instant, a loud roar sounded from the direction of the house, and a black and white sheep dog started up from his nap on the front steps and came barking toward her.

The sudden noise startled Janey, but she held her ground and watched the approaching dog with steady eyes. Straight at the stranger he came, still barking in deep and echoing thunders. However, Janey noticed that his plumed tail was moving in rapid circles, his ears were pricked up, and he flung his front paws forward in a joyous bounce. Before he had half reached her, she knew she wouldn't have to fear him.

As plain as day, the dog was saying to whoever might be in the house or barn: "There's a stranger here and you should know about it, but it's only a small girl who doesn't look harmful."

And as if in answer to that message, a door in the barn opened and a man stepped out. He looked about quickly, caught sight of Janey standing near the bridge with the dog sniffing around her, and lost no time in getting to her. Janey, intent on the dog, didn't look at the approaching man until he was within a few feet of her, and then she found herself meeting the shifty eyes of Bounce Reyburn.

"What are you doing here?" he demanded roughly.

"Nothing special," replied Janey with an amiable grin. "I'm just spying out the land."

To Bounce, who was not nearly so familiar with the Old Testament as was Janey, the word "spying" could mean only one thing.

"So you admit you're spying, eh?"

Janey nodded, never dreaming that Bounce could mean anything unpleasant.

"Well, it's a good thing Danger spotted you before you

found the hen house. Now get off the place and stay off of it, if you know what's good for you. We don't want people snoopin' around here."

Now Janey knew what he meant. He thought her a thief, the kind of person who would sneak into a chicken house and steal whatever she could find there. No one had ever called her a thief before, and for a moment she was too astonished to feel resentment. But only for a moment. Then her fists knotted at her sides, fury straightened her backbone until she seemed to grow inches in the next half-minute. And Bounce looked away quickly from the anger in her eyes.

"Don't you dare call me a thief!" she said, choking. "Don't you dare!"

The man simply grinned in amusement at Janey's outburst. "Never mind the play-actin'. You heard me! Git!"

This was too much. And without warning, the undersized, barefooted Janey became a small tempest of wrath. She flew at Bounce, hitting him wherever she could, and kicking at him with her bare toes. Danger circled them, barking wildly. Bounce, surprised at first by the sudden attack, fell back a step or two. But he quickly recovered himself, seized Janey's wrists, and held her, writhing helplessly, at arm's length.

Then it was that a new voice silenced Danger with a word, and in a calm tone asked: "What's going on here?"

Bounce dropped Janey's wrists as if they had been red hot. Janey pushed her hair back over her head, smoothed her hands along the sides of her overalls, and looked at the newcomer with smoldering eyes in which there was no trace of tears. She saw a tall, broad-shouldered man who might be a little older than her father. He wore a closely clipped gray mustache, and his brown eyes were glancing from Bounce to Janey with something suspiciously like a twinkle in their depths.

"What's going on here?" he repeated.

"Some of this cotton trash hangin' around lookin' for what they can pick up. I told her to git and she like to have had a fit."

"I am not a thief," protested Janey, "and I'll fight anybody that says I am, even you," she added defiantly to the newcomer.

"I don't blame you," he replied kindly. "Nobody wants to be called that. Where do you live?"

Janey pointed vaguely toward the west and said: "Over there." She wondered how this man could have appeared so suddenly, then noticed a sweaty saddle horse standing in the shade, its bridle reins trailing to the ground, and guessed that he must have ridden up just as she flew at Bounce.

"Did you come over here all alone?" queried the man.

"No." Janey shook her head. "Dad and Mom are asleep on the river bank. We came to fish. I caught the first one."

The stranger smiled at that.

"What's your name?"

"Janey Larkin. What's yours?"

"Anderson. Nils Anderson."

"Why," began Janey in happy astonishment, "then you're the one——"

But what she was about to say died on her lips. For some reason she could never have explained, she happened to glance at Bounce, and the look in his eyes silenced her and sent a shiver along her spine. She had seen the same ugly light there that had been in them on that night when Dad had demanded a receipt in payment of the rent.

"What were you going to say?" Mr. Anderson prompted her.

"Only that you're the one who owns all this land around here," Janey finished, again glancing at Bounce in time to catch his too wide grin. Bounce evidently didn't want Mr. Anderson to know she was living in his house. She wondered why, but at the same time was as determined as Bounce that Mr. Anderson should never find out. She would do nothing to risk their being allowed to stay there. Even though she liked this Mr. Anderson and disliked Bounce, she would follow Bounce's instructions. There was too much at stake to do otherwise.

At the same time she hated having to hide anything from Mr. Anderson. He seemed so willing to trust her, it was sneaky not to return his trust. Some instinct urged her to do so, but she could feel Bounce Reyburn's eyes upon her, and it was he who controlled her fortunes at the moment. One word, and she knew he would send the Larkin family packing. Janey couldn't risk that.

While she was turning all this over in her mind, the two men were studying her as if they were trying to decide what should be done with this small girl. But Janey, quite undisturbed by their scrutiny, simply dropped on one knee and snapped her fingers at the dog. Reassured, now that the visitor's presence was known and the master at hand, Danger slowly sauntered up to her, ears back and tail down. His whole attitude was apologetic, even humble, and such a sharp contrast to his previous one, that when he gravely lowered himself onto his haunches and offered his paw, Janey laughed and shook hands forgivingly with him.

"Why do you call him Danger?"

She had to tip her head far back to see into Mr. Anderson's face. It made her pointed chin look more elfin than usual, and her eyes, squinting against the light and still brimming with laughter, had an almost impish mischief in them.

"We call him Danger because there isn't the first thing dangerous about him," was the surprising answer. "He's a good friend and a discriminating one, too. You seem to get on with dogs, Janey. Do you have one?"

Janey lowered her head. "No," she said, then on sudden impulse added: "but we have a blue willow plate. It sort of takes the place of a dog, and a doll—and, oh, a lot of things."

She looked up again, shyly, wondering if Mr. Anderson would understand what she meant or whether he would be merely amused at what he considered a little girl's foolishness. But strangely enough, he looked very serious, as serious as if he had been listening to a grown-up. Encouraged, Janey continued:

"It belonged to my great-great-grandmother. And it has a picture on it of a bridge and a willow and three people, and other things besides."

Suddenly Janey stopped. She straightened up and glanced quickly about her. Now she knew why this place had seemed familiar to her. It was the same as the willow plate—well, almost the same. The bridge, the willow trees, the house, even the three of them standing there. Of course, the bridge was not an arched bridge, the house was not a Chinese house, and neither were the three of them quite like the people in the story, although it would be easy to imagine Bounce in the role of cruel father. But it was enough like the blue willow plate to make Janey wonder if fairy tales ever came true. Perhaps at the very least it could be considered a good omen. She had heard about such things. Of one thing she was certain: Mr. Anderson's dooryard was as familiar to her as the willow plate, and for one mixed-up moment she couldn't have told which she had known first.

She realized all at once that the two men were talking and that the talk concerned her, so she stifled her excitement to pay attention to what was being said.

Mr. Anderson was speaking. "I think we ought to square ourselves with Janey for hurting her feelings." There was an unmistakable twinkle in his eye. "Do you think, Janey, you would feel a little better about things if Bounce gave you a paper bag, escorted you to the hen house, and let you choose a dozen eggs to take away with you?"

Janey took a moment to think this over. It would be nice to have the eggs; they would be a real treat. But it was Bounce who had called her a thief and he probably still considered her one. She didn't want to accept anything from his hands, not even when it was really offered by somebody else. Still, Mr. Anderson wanted to be kind, and they hadn't had eggs for quite a long time.

"Yes," she said at last, holding her head proudly and looking almost angrily at Mr. Anderson. "I'll take the eggs, but if you'll tell me where the hen house is, I'd rather go for them alone."

Bounce snickered rudely. "Don't get your hopes up, kid. It won't be a very big bag."

"That's enough of that kind of talk." Mr. Anderson spoke sharply and his face was set and hard. "You know a lot more about cattle than you do people, Bounce. There's something in this child's ancestry you couldn't even begin to understand. Let her help herself. Good-by, Janey," he ended abruptly, and walked away before she had a chance to thank him.

So Janey spied out the land and returned to Dad and Mom, not with grapes and pomegranates, but with a dozen fresh and creamy-colored eggs. And before they returned home, they caught five more catfish.

On her way to bed that night, Janey paused for a glimpse of the willow plate. Somehow it seemed lovelier than ever and much more precious. A few moments later, lying on her makeshift bed, she watched a tiny light move across the dark dome of sky framed in the doorway. It reminded her of the hawk that was like a lost shadow. Was this a star that had lost its way? But the light moved more purposely than anything lost would do, and Janey knew it was the northbound passenger plane. It passed among the stars and out of sight, leaving her to think back over this day. More than ever she wanted to stay here, and not only because of Lupe, important as her friendship had become. Since her discovery of the Anderson dooryard, a definite and thrilling conviction had taken possession of Janey's heart. With that strange visit, the wish to stay had become more than a mere wish. It had become an obligation. Because, beyond the slightest doubt, Janey knew that this was where the willow plate belonged.

5. CAMP MILLER SCHOOL

JANEY AND DAD WERE ON THEIR WAY TO THE COTTON FIELDS.
Dad was going to work; Janey was going to school. It was
October now. The sun, though bright and warm, was not hot
as it had been a month ago, and the mountains, as if reward-
ing the valley for milder weather, were allowing their blue
outlines to be seen. Wild sunflowers turned bright faces to
the east, and occasional dust devils went spiraling off across
the plain in merry abandon. But Janey, huddled in a corner
of the ragged front seat, was sulkily indifferent to the world
around her. The corners of her mouth sagged, her lower lip

85

protruded in something close to a pout, and her eyes glow-
ered darkly. She wasn't glad to be going to school, not this
school at any rate. If only she were being taken to the town
school, the one where Lupe and all the other children of the
district went! That is, they did if they belonged to the district. Janey was well aware that actually she herself could
have attended that school, too. There was no law forbidding
it. But it was a fact, too, that in some communities she would
have been extremely unwelcome, and Dad, knowing this,
had made his own law in respect to Janey.

"We'll keep with our own kind," he had once said when she
had remonstrated with him. "The camp schools are put there
for us to use and so we'll use them and be thankful. Besides,
a body can learn anywhere if he's a mind to."

Janey hadn't argued further with him on that occasion and
she had no desire to do so today. She knew that going to the
"regular" school would no longer satisfy her anyway, for just
going there couldn't make her really belong. Since she had
begun to want to stay in this place, merely going to the district school was no longer enough. What Janey wanted was
to belong to this place and to go to the district school because
as a member of the community it was her right to go there.
The camp school would now be a daily and forceful reminder
of the fact that she didn't belong, and so she dreaded it.

She knew what the camp school would be like. No two of
the children would have learned the same things, and it
would all be a jumble. In some lessons, Janey would find herself way ahead of most of the boys and girls her age, and she
would be expected as a matter of course to know other things

she had never had a chance to learn. Most of the time she wouldn't know whether she was going or coming and there would be endless questions and much tiresome fussing.

Besides, it was much too early in the day for school to start and she would have to wait around until it did. She would have asked Dad to let her go into the field with him if she had thought it would do any good. But she knew from past experience that it wouldn't. Never had she been allowed to do any field work. Other children did and sometimes Mom, but never Janey. Dad, so easy-going about most things, was firm on this. So Janey sat with a frown on her face as the old car jolted along its way, and came very near to feeling sorry for herself.

She would have known the school house as soon as they came in sight of it even if Dad hadn't bothered to point it out. She had seen many of them before and they all looked alike. Some were newer than others and that was about the only difference. This was one of the newer ones. It was a rather large square building, its unpainted boards gleaming in the bright light. In front of it a flagpole, also unpainted, towered against the morning sky. As yet no flag was in evidence, so Janey knew for sure that school had not yet started. Her father let her off at the front steps, then drove over to park beside a row of cars that looked as if they might all have come from the same junk pile. Janey sat down to wait, her package of lunch beside her.

Across from her were the cottages, row upon row, that comprised the camp. Looking at these little one-room sheds so close together that their eaves almost touched, she was thankful for their own shack and the spreading country around it. Of course there was plenty of country spread around here. But the camp itself was squeezed into as small a space as possible so as not to use up any more of the cotton ground than was absolutely necessary. The deep green of the cotton plants reached in every direction almost as far as the eye could see. And here and there against the green of every bush a gleam of white showed clearly. That was where a cotton boll had burst open to free the fluffy fibers which would be picked by hand from each boll. There would be thousands, perhaps millions, of these little white bunches and it would take many fingers working many hours a day to pick all the ripening cotton. That is why there was a village of little houses at this place with a school house at hand. During the picking season hundreds of people lived here and worked here until the day should come when all the cotton was harvested. Then they would load their cars with what household goods they owned, and with their boys and girls the cotton pickers would move on to some other part of the country which needed their hands and their heads.

Of course, Janey wasn't thinking of all this while she sat on the steps of the school house. It was so much a part of her life that she didn't bother to think about it any more than she bothered to think about the processes of breathing when she drew fresh air into her lungs.

For perhaps ten minutes, Janey sat there, a blue-overalled figure of gloom, when all at once she caught a movement in the dust in front of her. It was so slight a movement that at first she thought her eyes were playing her tricks. But in the

next second, the dust was again stirred, and then she was off
the school house steps in one lunge. Flat on the ground she
hurled herself, one arm reaching out ahead of her. Slowly she
drew in her arm, her hand tightly closed, and gathered herself up. From head to foot she was coated with fine dirt, but
she didn't care. She didn't even stop to brush herself off before she slowly began to open her fingers, squinting closely at
what she held there. A smile widened across her face, for in
the shadowy hollow of her palm was a small horned toad.
Its eyes, mere pinheads of glistening black, stared fiercely at
her, and its chinless mouth was set grimly. But Janey was not
alarmed. She had captured many horned toads before this
and knew that for all their fierce expression and spiky covering, they were quite harmless creatures. Slowly she lowered
herself onto the school house steps once more to inspect her
captive. To most people he would have appeared far from
beautiful, but to Janey he seemed an object of delight. His
four tiny feet with their minute claws were perfect, and from
the fringe of miniature scales outlining what should have
been his chin, to the last infinitesimal spike on the end of his
brief tail, he was finished and complete. Janey loved him
at once and began cautiously to draw her finger across his
hard little head.

Suddenly an idea occurred to her. She would use this
horned toad to test the new teacher. In every school she had
ever been, someone had always solemnly assured her whenever she happened to mention a "horned toad" that she
should call them "horned lizards," for they were not really
toads at all. Janey had always been entirely willing to accept

the fact that they were not, strictly speaking, "horned toads," but to call them anything else just wasn't possible. The minute you said "horned lizard" you turned a perfectly good horned toad into a new and unattractive animal. She would loathe having anyone refer to her new pet as a horned lizard, and if the new teacher did so, Janey's respect for her as a human being would be completely shattered. It would be, she thought, like saying "It is I" instead of "It's me." If you used the former, you would be correct, but you wouldn't be a friend. She was determined to discover whether the new teacher was a friend or merely correct.

She and the horned toad had not long to wait. Janey had hardly got some of the dirt brushed off when a dusty sedan rolled to a halt in the shade of the school house and a fat and smiling woman got out of it. Janey felt hopeful.

"Hello," called the woman. "No ten-o'clock-scholar about you, is there?"

Janey felt increasingly hopeful as she rose to meet this stranger who was undoubtedly the teacher. Surely no one who quoted Mother Goose to you before she had asked your name would call a horned toad a horned lizard. More than that, she would know what to do with you if you were good in reading and poor in arithmetic. Suddenly the whole tone of the day was changed. But the final test was yet to come.

"Look," said Janey, holding out her captive.

"Well, bless my soul," said the woman heartily, bending over Janey's hand, "a horned toad! Did you catch it?"

Janey nodded, too delighted for the moment to speak, then: "But I haven't named him yet."

"Can't let him go without a name. Let's see." The woman thought a moment. Then, "I have it. Let's call him Fafnir. He was a first-class dragon when giants ruled the earth. And this fellow looks a lot like a dragon. A fairy dragon. Does Fafnir appeal to you?"

Janey nodded.

The teacher chuckled. "I suppose the proper thing would be to let the horned toad decide such an important matter for himself. But from the look of him I should say that he wasn't quite on speaking terms with us yet."

She looked at Janey with eyes that were merry and direct. Trustworthy eyes with friendly secrets in their depths.

"I am Miss Peterson," she said.

"I'm Janey Larkin."

A stout arm encircled Janey's narrow shoulders and for a brief moment she felt herself squeezed against Miss Peterson's warm and well-cushioned side.

"Welcome to Camp Miller school, Janey. Come on inside. We'll start the day together."

No questions, no fussing. Just "Come on in," as if she had known you always. Janey slid an arm around Miss Peterson's ample waist and together they entered the building, the small girl walking on tiptoe, to her teacher's secret amusement. Miss Peterson would have been surprised to know she was the innocent cause of that strange behavior. For Janey was thrilling to the certainty that this very morning, unexpectedly and alone, she had discovered the most wonderful teacher in the world. That was enough to make anyone prance on tiptoe! A few minutes ago she had been feeling sorry for herself and all the time there had been Fafnir and Miss Peterson. Not even Lupe going to the "regular" school could possibly have enjoyed such luck as that!

During the next half-hour Janey helped Miss Peterson prepare for the day's work. She cleaned the blackboards and put the tables and benches in order. Some pink petunias were blooming in a window box and Janey watered them from the standing pipe outside the door. Then she picked off the withered blossoms, which left her fingers so sticky she had to return to the water pipe to wash her hands. Soon the boys and girls began to arrive. The school day started at nine o'clock when one of the boys carried the flag out to the unpainted pole and fastened it to the rope neatly secured there. While the whole school stood grouped at attention, the flag was drawn slowly up into the morning sky until at last it came to rest at the pole's very top and the Stars and Stripes was unfolded above the school and the camp. The little ceremony ended, they all trooped to their lessons.

As the morning advanced, Janey's regard for Miss Peterson increased, if that were possible. Because they were crowded on the benches, and because their legs were not all long enough to reach the floor, she saw to it that the children were given time to move around and rest. And it seemed to be the custom for two or three of the children to tell the others each day which part of the country they had thought the most interesting in their traveling around. Janey, listening to the others this morning, decided, when her turn came, to tell about the place by the river which she had discovered the other day. The place like the willow plate.

Right in the midst of one of these recitals, there was a sudden disturbance outside. A covered truck stopped in front of the door, and Miss Peterson's face seemed to light up at the sight of it. She stopped the boy who was talking, and said to the room: "This is our lucky day. The library people are here." But though she sounded as if it were something especially fine, none of the boys and girls appeared interested. And this was not surprising, since none of them knew who "library people" were.

Two women came into the room and Miss Peterson shook hands with them. Janey eyed them with curiosity, and all at once she had the strange feeling that one of them she had seen before. But it wasn't possible. She didn't know anyone around here except the Romeros, and of course Bounce Reyburn and Mr. Anderson. Yet one of those faces was very familiar in a haunting, ghostly way. Miss Peterson turned to the class.

"Miss Adams and Miss Gray have brought us some books," she announced, "and we'll have recess while I pick them out."

Immediately the children wiggled off their benches and filed out, their curious eyes fixed on the newcomers. And then Janey knew where she had seen that face before. Miss Adams had been the person in the booth at the fair, the booth full of books for boys and girls! She had brought books out to them. Janey wondered excitedly if these books would be new and shiny like those at the fair.

Outside, the boys circled the truck, their glances frankly admiring. That was the sort of thing to travel around in. Lots of room. Janey wasn't interested in the truck, but she hung around in the hope of seeing what sort of books were coming out of it. She could hardly wait for the library people to go, so great was her eagerness to see what they would leave behind them.

But when they had finally gone, Janey's high hopes were abruptly dashed. The books were old and ragged, with some of the pictures torn out. But they were all good stories, she discovered on looking them over. Many of them she recognized as titles she had seen at the fair. And once upon a time they had been new. Janey picked up a copy of *King Arthur* because its "thee's" and "thou's" looked comfortably familiar, and returned to her bench with it. As she opened the book's worn cover, she tried very hard to remember that in the beginning it, too, had been new and shiny. Then she began to read, and forgot everything but the shining splendor of its pages.

When school was over for the day—it ended sooner than most schools, for the boys and girls worked in the cotton— they again went out to the flagpole and lowered the colors. Somehow the whole place looked dingier after the flag had been put away. Janey walked into the cotton patch and let Fafnir go. He had had an exciting day and it would be cruel to keep the tiny captive longer. Besides, horned toads were fairly plentiful; she could catch another Fafnir almost any time. Then she curled up in the shade, her back resting against the school house wall, to wait for Dad. She knew she would have to wait a long time but now she didn't care. Miss Peterson had let her keep *King Arthur* until tomorrow.

Her father had been grinning down at her for several seconds before Janey became aware of him. She looked up, startled to find Dad instead of a knight in armor standing before her.

"Think you can get your nose out of that long enough to ride home with me?" he asked.

Without answering, she got dreamily to her feet, serenity on her face and quiet dignity in her bearing. The spell of *King Arthur* still held Janey and she moved quietly so as not to shatter it. For the moment, the blue-overalled little girl on the edge of the cotton patch had become the Lady Guinevere, while the man beside her had assumed the figure of the noblest knight in Christendom.

But as they reached the row of parked cars, Janey became herself again. It was beyond even her power to imagine the Lady Guinevere climbing into an automobile.

"I wish we lived back in olden times when lovely ladies lived in castles and brave knights in shining armor went around defending them," Janey remarked as Dad backed the car around.

"Well, you seem like a pretty lovely lady to me," he replied, "even if you don't exactly live in a castle. And I'll defend you willingly whenever it's necessary."

Janey looked annoyed. "Yes, I know. But that isn't what I mean. In those days everything was an adventure and you just had to be brave or it was the end of you."

Dad was silent for so long following her words that Janey glanced at him and was surprised to discover a sober expression on his face. The teasing smile was gone entirely. Had she said something wrong? She waited a little anxiously for him to speak.

At last, he cleared his throat and began to talk, his hands tightening on the steering wheel, and his eyes straight before him.

"Some day, Janey, perhaps when you're grown up, you'll realize that every day you've been living these last five years has been an adventure. You know, an adventure is just something that comes along that's unexpected and you don't know for sure how it will turn out. Sometimes there may be danger mixed up in it. And it doesn't matter whether it happened a thousand years ago or right this minute. It's still an adventure. Every day that comes along is an adventure to us, and may be dangerous because we don't know for sure what it's going to bring. Perhaps I'm wrong, but I've got a hunch that it takes just about as much courage to live like that without losing your grip on things as ever it took to buckle on armor and go out to fight some fellow who had a grudge against you."

Janey, listening attentively, weighed Dad's words and found them very puzzling. It was hard to discover anything adventurous in the way they lived. Her notions of adventure were quite different. She looked at Dad with carefully appraising eyes, trying to see in his seamed and sun-tanned face the look of a hero, and failed. It was a kind face and the dearest one in the world to her, but she had to admit in spite of her loyalty that Dad in a helmet and visor would have looked queer rather than noble.

It required, too, considerable effort for her to think of him as being brave. Yet she supposed he must be, since he had just said it took courage to live the kind of life they lived without losing your grip on things. Certainly Dad hadn't yet lost his grip. When the car broke down, as it frequently did, he simply went quietly about the business of fixing it. And after a long day in the fields he was never too tired to tease her when he came home. But was this really being brave? Janey hardly thought so. Still, Dad had as much as said it was, and Dad couldn't be wrong.

Then a surprising thought occurred to her. Why, she and Mom must be brave too, since they were living the same kind of life. That settled it. Dad was wrong, after all. She was dead certain that whatever other qualities she might possess, bravery was not one of them. And she doubted if Mom was truly brave, either. Dad, perhaps. But she and Mom, never. What had Dad meant? Could there be more than one kind of courage in the world? Janey considered this possibility for a moment, but found it too confusing.

"I guess I won't understand it till I'm grown up," she thought comfortably, and was relieved when Dad asked her to tell him what had happened at school that day. For the rest of the ride home, Fafnir and Miss Peterson crowded all other topics out of the conversation.

6. THE CONTEST

THOUGH IT WAS BARELY SIX O'CLOCK IN THE MORNING, THE Larkin shack was in a fever of activity. Most of it was caused by Janey, who kept running out to peer at the sky and to rush back with the report that "There isn't a cloud as big as my hand anywhere. It isn't going to rain after all, and I'm glad, I'm glad, because rain would spoil everything."

"You'd better calm down and eat your breakfast or we won't get around in time to go with your father," Mrs. Larkin warned her, and Janey finally paused at the table long enough to eat her portion of fried salt pork and corn bread.

She had good reason to be excited, for this was the day of the Wasco County Cotton Picking Contest. All the pickers who had qualified by making a record of more than three hundred pounds of cotton picked in a single day were to vie with one another for first places in the picking contest. Mr. Larkin had qualified, along with seventy-five others, and at seven o'clock would go to the field to start the nine hours of grueling work in an effort to win one of the cash prizes. And the prizes were worth working for. If he won first place, he would receive one hundred and twenty-five dollars, in addition to which he would be paid the regular wage of ninety cents a hundred pounds for the actual picking. If he won second place, he would claim seventy-five dollars, and third would bring fifty dollars. There were lesser amounts for fourth, fifth, and sixth places, but Janey hadn't bothered to consider them. Dad couldn't rate less than third. Suppose he should come in first! They would be almost rich. Janey paused with her mouth full of corn bread to speculate on the things that one hundred and twenty-five dollars would bring them, and so alluring were the splendors before her mind's eye, that she might have sat there the rest of the morning if Mrs. Larkin hadn't goaded her again into making haste.

Across the road, there was a light in the Romero house. Every picker was allowed a swamper, or helper, and Mr. Larkin had asked Manuel Romero to assist him. It was agreed that if he won either of the first three prizes, Manuel would receive ten dollars for his work, five dollars if Mr. Larkin came in fourth, fifth, or sixth, and nothing at all if he lost altogether. Manuel was quite willing to take his chances with his neighbor. Both families were to attend the contest in a body. To Janey, it was the most exciting thing that had ever happened to them. Never before had Dad competed in such a contest, and her anxiety over the outcome was almost more than she could stand.

"Oh, Dad," she stopped to exclaim as they were going out the door, "suppose you don't win anything at all!"

Until this moment she had never seriously considered such a possibility. But now that the time for starting was actually here, the ugly thought would intrude itself in spite of all she could do to push it from her.

"Suppose you don't win anything at all?" she repeated.

"Well, in that case, I'll have my day's wages, and at the rate I'm going to pick that won't be anything to sneeze at."

Janey giggled, feeling better at once. Dad had such a funny way of saying things sometimes. Of course he'd win. First place too, more than likely. She had been silly to think anything else even for a minute.

But later, as with Lupe she walked to the edge of the field where the pickers were spread out awaiting the starting gun, she again felt a slight qualm of doubt. Seventy-six men stood there, each facing a row of gleaming cotton, Dad with the rest, his long picking sack around his waist and trailing out for several feet behind him. Somehow, Dad looked awfully like just anybody. He didn't look a bit like the best cotton picker in Wasco County. But then, neither did any of the others. They looked like very ordinary men, their stature dwarfed a little by that wide field. But their eyes had a new eagerness this morning, and their faces were strangely alert.

A newcomer dropped suddenly into that place would have known instantly something important was about to happen.

It was a perfect autumn day with a little mistiness on the horizon which the climbing sun had not yet shone away. The blue bowl of the sky fitted neatly onto the edge of the reaching land with no ragged edges to show where land and sky were joined unless you counted the distant blue willows where the river ran. There was a hush over everything, for voices were swallowed up in that vast space, and when the gun cracked to announce the start of the contest, it sounded more like the bark of a toy pistol than a real gun. But as one man, the pickers bent to their work, so Janey decided it was a real gun she had heard. She left Lupe and sidled up beside Mrs. Larkin, slipping a hand into hers.

"Oh, Mom, I do so terribly want Dad to win. Do you think he will?"

Mrs. Larkin held Janey's hand close and watched the pickers for a few seconds before she replied, and then she said slowly: "Nobody knows, daughter. He'll just have to do the best he can and take his chances with the rest. I guess that's the way all life is, mostly."

Janey pondered the sober words, sensing rather than realizing a great wisdom in them. They were almost like words she had come on in the Bible. Mom talked like that sometimes. And sometimes, as now, she seemed far off, like God. You never thought of teasing or playing with Mom the way you did with Dad. Mom was different. She it was who made you do the things you should and spoke words that made you think. There were things close locked in Mom that Janey had longed lately to discover, and felt sure she never would. But Janey knew that without her she and Dad would be as useless as cotton plants without the sun.

The men had picked down the long rows, weighed in and dumped their bags of cotton, and were working back to the place from which they had started. Janey and Lupe ran to meet them. More and more people had come to watch the picking, crowds were following the men, and traffic officers had arrived to keep the onlookers from hindering the workers.

Lupe moved away from one burly officer, eying with suspicion the gun swinging at his hip.

"Come on," said Janey impatiently, "what are you afraid of?"

"Him," with a nod toward the officer.

"Afraid of a motor cop?" asked Janey, in amazement. "He won't hurt you. Lots of times when the car gets something wrong with it and we get stuck on the road, a motor cop comes along and tries to help us fix it."

"They arrest people," declared Lupe firmly.

"Sure they do when you're breaking a law, or something. But they're all right, honest." Janey was a little disgusted with Lupe.

"I betcha you're a-scared to go up and say something to him," challenged Lupe, still doubtful in spite of Janey's reassurances.

"I am not," replied Janey, coming down hard on the last word, and striking out to where the officer in question was chatting with a knot of sightseers.

Janey waited until she caught his eye, and grinned at him.

"Hello, young sprout, how's tricks?" he demanded.

"My dad's in the contest," announced Janey.

"No foolin'?" asked the officer. "Which one is he?"

"That one." Janey flung out an arm, and moved closer to the officer. Out of the tail of her eye, she could see Lupe approaching cautiously.

"So, that's your dad? Say, he's no slouch. I've been watching him for the last few minutes and he can sure pick cotton."

At this, Janey longed to throw her arms around the officer's sunburned neck, but wasn't quite sure such an action would be within the law. Instead she just beamed happily, and trotted along beside him as he started down the field. Lupe came trotting along behind.

Suddenly, without warning, the officer stopped in his long stride and the little Mexican girl ran smack into him.

"Hey, what's going on here?" he cried, grabbing her by the shoulders and grinning down into her scared face. "Tryin' to rush me, or something?"

Poor Lupe. It was well that the man was holding her in a firm grip or she would have fallen to the ground, for her legs were limp under her. Her eyes were enormous pools of black terror in her graying face and she looked as if her last minute had come. Janey could hardly keep from laughing, but liked Lupe too well to ridicule her thus openly. Instead, she said:

"Lupe's afraid of cops, but she shouldn't be, should she?"

"Heck, no," replied the officer. "I've got two kids at home

and I'll tell you something if you promise not to breathe it
to a soul." He released Lupe and gave a quick look around
as if he were actually afraid someone might overhear him.
The two little girls bent close. "Those kids of mine don't mind
me worth a cent," confessed the big man, "but don't you ever
let that out. Now skedaddle, I've got work to do."

"You see," said Janey, as she watched the broad back with
its Sam Browne belt drawing away from them, "you see.
Cops aren't anything to be afraid of."

But Lupe still looked a little unconvinced.

The hours dragged on, the sun rode high in the heavens,
and still the men's swift fingers moved over the green plants,
sweeping the cotton into the picking sacks. Time and time
again the sacks were weighed and their fluffy contents
dumped into the trucks until their high sides bulged with
the snowy loads. The pickers snatched a hasty lunch, hardly
halting in their work, and the afternoon wore on. The final
outcome of the race could be guessed at now. Mr. Larkin
was well in the lead of most of the field. Only one man
seemed to challenge his chances at first place. This one was
a huge Negro whose big black hands moved with unerring
deftness and with lightning speed. Good-naturedly he
chaffed at his white rival whenever they were within hailing
distance of each other, and Mr. Larkin replied in kind.

Janey, almost worn out with the day's excitement, was sitting with Lupe in the Larkin car.

"What would you do if you had a thousand dollars?"
Janey asked suddenly.

Money prizes had occupied so much of her mind all day that now it was easy to let her dreams of wealth lift her thoughts above mere possible sums to wholly fantastic amounts.

Lupe took a moment to consider the question, then answered: "If I had a thousand dollars, I'd buy an automobile. It would be light yellow with shining wheels. And it would have red leather on the inside, and two horns. And I'd drive it anytime I wanted to."

Lupe's eyes fairly glowed as she contemplated the splendid vision. Janey glanced at her with surprise and satisfaction. It was something to have discovered there were things in Lupe's mind that weren't just everyday things, even if they were only yellow automobiles. And Lupe rose further in her regard when she continued the game by asking: "What would you do?"

Janey's answer was ready.

"I'd have a house built with rooms in it for all of us, not counting the kitchen. And it would be all light inside and clean, and there would be water pipes right inside the house, so you could just turn them off and on whenever you wanted to. And on one of the walls there would be a shelf for the willow plate, and we would stay in it always and . . ."

But what further wonders Janey's dream house was to have remained forever a mystery, for just then a gun went off for the second time that day. The contest was over.

Pell-mell, the two girls scrambled out of the car and began racing for the field. A crowd was gathering swiftly around the trucks, tired men running jerkily from the field if they were sure they had placed somewhere near the top. The others came more slowly to claim their day's wages.

In a few minutes the tension would be ended and the prize money paid out. Janey saw her father with Manuel Romero at his side standing in a group of men while the weights were being checked. The crowd was quiet, eager to catch the first word of the results. At last it came. A name was called out, a shout went up and the big colored man stepped forward, his sweating face split by a wide and gleaming smile. So Dad hadn't won first place after all. For a moment Janey felt as if she must run away, as if she couldn't endure the strain of waiting for the other results. She looked toward her father and wondered how he could appear so calm and could go on talking quietly with Manuel just as if this were no different from the end of any other day's work. But even as she watched him, she heard another name called. It sounded like "Larkin," only she might have been mistaken. But no, now Dad was moving forward, and men were slapping him on the back. It was, it was Larkin. Dad had won second place and seventy-five dollars!

Janey didn't know she had been leaping up and down until she felt a hand on her shoulder. "You'll thump yourself right down to China if you keep that up." Janey looked up to see Mom smiling down at her. Actually smiling.

"Oh, Mom!" cried Janey, flinging both arms around her waist and pressing her face against her. "I'm afraid I'll *bust*."

"It wouldn't surprise me a bit if you went off, just like a firecracker," came the calm voice above her. "Here comes your father; we'd better start for the car."

The next day Mr. Larkin, instead of going to work, took his family into Fresno to make some much-needed purchases now that there was a little extra money at hand. First of all, the car needed four new tires. Of course they wouldn't be brand-new ones, but at the second-hand dealers' they would find some that were much better than those already on the wheels, and these must be found before any other things were bought. For with a family like the Larkins, a car was the most important thing they owned. Without it, their means of earning a livelihood would be at an end, since everything depended on their ability to keep up with the harvests. Without a car in fairly good operating condition, they would be helpless. Janey understood this quite as well as her father and mother and only permitted herself to hope a little wistfully as they rolled along the highway that there would be something left over after the tires were bought. Janey wanted a new coat.

As they crossed the bridge her eyes were alert to catch a glimpse of the Anderson place on the other side of the river. It was easy to recognize the grove of trees that marked the ranch house but the buildings showed only in brief flashes as they drove past, since the trees and shrubbery almost screened them from the highway, and they were set well back from the road.

There had been no time for picnicking after that one excursion, and, except that the memory of it was as clear as the morning, Janey might have thought she had dreamed that scene under the willows when a dog called Danger had barked at her and a man named Mr. Anderson had taken her part. Bounce had appeared at the shack once since that time to collect the rent. Janey very much resented having Bounce a part of the Anderson place, the place that was like the willow plate. Now the ranch and the plate had become so nearly one in her thoughts that she couldn't separate them. To think of one, was to summon the other to her mind's eye. And for the first time in her life there was something unpleasant mixed with her happiness in thinking of the willow plate. That something was Bounce.

But then you couldn't expect to have everything, Janey reasoned, sensibly. Right now they were on their way to town with at least seventy-five dollars in the buckskin bag. The day was bright and so far the car was behaving perfectly. Not even a Bounce Reyburn could cloud the luster of this day's splendid beginning. If only there would be a little money left over from the tires!

It took nearly two hours to buy the tires. Janey hadn't realized there were so many second-hand tire shops in the world, and Mr. Larkin called at every one of them and bargained carefully before finally making up his mind to do business. Then there was further delay while the old tires were removed and the others, which the man assured them were practically as good as new, were installed. By that time it was nearly noon and Janey was good and hungry.

"Let's leave the car right here, and do the rest of our shopping on foot," Dad suggested.

"Might as well," Mom seconded, and so they did.

Janey couldn't remember when she had last walked along a street like this with automobiles coming and going and street cars clanging past. There were windows so filled with fascinating things she almost forgot she was hungry until suddenly the fragrance of cooked food was wafted to her as a man swung open the door of a restaurant just ahead of them and stepped out onto the street. Coming abreast of the place, Janey flattened her nose against the large front window and peered inside. She saw a long counter with stools in front of it and white-uniformed women setting plates of steaming food before waiting customers. It all looked simply delicious and Janey longed to go inside. Just then she heard Dad's voice behind her and could hardly believe her ears.

"What do you say we go inside and sample their stuff?" he was saying.

With one bound Janey was through the door and wriggling onto a stool before the long counter. A waitress slapped a menu down before her and Janey lost herself in the long list of delectable foods which on this day were being offered. Never had she read anything more interesting than that menu. Once, twice, thrice she went down the list. It was as thrilling as *King Arthur* and the Bible all rolled into one. She heard Dad give his order, then Mom. Now it was her turn; the waitress was standing impatiently before her, pencil poised, and still Janey couldn't make up her mind. Should she have roast beef and mashed potatoes, or veal stew with "homemade" noodles?

"Come, come," said Mom at last, "name one and look at the rest. We can't stay here all day."

"Roast beef," said Janey and sighed. For the rest of the day she would be regretting that veal stew. If only she had room enough and time enough and money enough to eat it all! To start right at the top of the menu card and eat her way clear to the bottom! It would be wonderful!

But the roast beef when it came was so good that Janey forgot all about the other things, and when they had finished and Dad paid the bill she was further gratified to observe that there were still quite a few pieces of currency left in the buckskin bag.

Once again they began to walk along the noisy street until they came to a large store with windows jammed full of all sorts of things. There were clothes to wear and pots to cook in and even chairs to sit in all mixed up together in a nice convenient way so that you could see at a glance just what the store had to offer. And everything in the window had a neat sign on it stating exactly just what each thing cost.

Into this store went Mr. and Mrs. Larkin with Janey close at their heels. Now Mom had paused at a counter and was asking a question of the young lady behind it, and the young lady was nodding toward a far corner of the store. Janey hadn't tried to overhear what they said, but she couldn't help catching the word "coat," and now the young lady was smiling down at her in a special knowing sort of way. And Janey's head began to spin with a high hope. Breathlessly she followed in the wake of Dad and Mom as they sauntered slowly in the direction the clerk had indicated. And now there could be no doubt. They had arrived at the corner at last and there before Janey's dancing blue eyes were rows upon rows of tall racks with dozens upon dozens of coats hanging from them and every coat had been made to fit some little girl.

A clerk was coming toward them with eyebrows lifted in a politely questioning way. With a practiced, sweeping glance she took in Janey's skinny form, the dress just barely reaching to her knees and the sleeves of her shabby jacket ending two inches above her wrists.

"We want a coat for this girl," Mom was saying. "Something under ten dollars."

The clerk moved toward a rack. "These are eight-seventy-five," she said; "you'll find them a real value at that price."

Dad turned to Janey. "There you are, young one," he said. "Take your pick."

But it wasn't as simple as all that. No, indeed. Janey went around and around the rack, trying first to decide on the color. At length she settled on blue. Then she had to try on one after another to decide which style she liked best, and when that hurdle had been safely got over, they had to find one that was large enough to allow her to grow into it during the next few years, and still not so large that she would look ridiculous in it now. Finally a compromise was reached and Janey became the proud owner of a blue woolly new coat that came way down below her knees and well down over her hands, but which was warm and, to her eyes at least, beautiful.

After buying a few more things, such as overalls and shirts, quite unexciting, they started for home. They had managed well, for the car had new, or almost new, tires, Janey had a brand-new coat, and there was still some money left over in the buckskin bag.

7. WILD WINGS AND TROUBLE

THREE WEEKS HAD PASSED SINCE THE CONTEST AND A CHANGE
had come over the valley. The sunflowers had vanished from
the roadside, leaving only their tall and withered stalks jerk-
ing stiffly in the frequent south winds to remind one that
their jolly faces had ever cheered a passer-by. The tarweed
had bloomed and gone, and the tumbleweed, relinquishing
its hold upon the earth, now made good its name by rolling
along splendidly in whichever direction the wind blew, halting only when some fence stood in its path. The greasewood
alone seemed unaffected by the changing seasons.

To the west, the mountains were a low and clearly etched blue line. Often mighty cloud banks billowed up behind them and leaned out over them into the limitless sky. Watching the clouds gather, Janey wondered sometimes if there ever could be enough of them to cover that sky. But one day she discovered there were plenty and to spare. That day it rained. It was the first rain of the season and the thirsty ground drank up the moisture greedily. It was good to hear it pattering on the shingles of the roof, even if the roof did leak and Mrs. Larkin was forced to stand the washtub in the middle of the room. Even the sound of it striking the tub was a merry sound. Janey ran outside and tipped her face up to the raindrops, laughing as they splashed against her closed eyelids. Her thin little chest swelled to the bursting point as she drew the strong sweet smell of the wet earth deep into her lungs.

The red cattle in the field next door stopped their grazing and stood away from the wind, gazing vacantly into space. Rain or shine, it seemed to be all the same to them. Janey, alive to the sound and the scent and the feel of the rain, threw them a look of scorn. It was better, much better, she thought, to live in a leaky shack and to be hungry sometimes than to be as they were, unfeeling and unknowing of what was happening in the world. But she had to admit that their red coats dotted across the plain were a pleasant sight in the storm. Cows came in nice colors, she decided, as she turned to go back into the house.

The next day, the sun shone clear and there was a nip in the air. While the Larkins were still at breakfast, Manuel

Romero came over to announce that a certain rancher for whom he had worked that summer had some eucalyptus trees he wanted topped, and if Mr. Larkin cared to help him with the job, he could have half of the wood they would cut away.

"One good turn deserves another," said Manuel with his shy grin. He was referring, of course, to the ten dollars he had earned as Mr. Larkin's swamper during the contest.

This was very good news, for it meant that with a wood pile in the back yard, it would no longer be necessary for the Larkins to search the plain in ever-widening circles for greasewood stumps. It would mean, too, that today Janey would miss school, for Dad wouldn't be going to the field. Ordinarily she would have been sorry to miss school. Her admiration for Miss Peterson had grown to such an extent that there were moments when she almost forgot she had ever wanted to go to the "regular" school. But today Janey had a special reason for wanting to stay home.

For the past week, she had noticed occasionally against the sky undulating, parallel flights of birds which she knew were wild ducks. On whistling wings, they were sweeping in out of the north to settle on the slough which lay half a mile from the shack, the slough near the highway where the red-winged blackbirds had swung on tule reeds that far-off day when Janey had gone to the fair with the Romero family. For days she had longed to steal away to where the wild ducks were. Every autumn since she was old enough to care about such things, she had awaited the arrival of these birds as one awaits the coming of a well-loved friend. To Janey they seemed friends. Wherever she had happened to be, always in the fall, the ducks had come to her. And now in this San Joaquin Valley they were coming again. In her uncertain life with its constant shifts and changes, the faithful reappearance of the wild ducks each fall gave her the feeling of something solid and sure. In a world where everything was topsy-turvy and nothing was certain from one day to the next, here was one thing that was dependable and unfailing. For a week she had watched them fly in, now today she would go to where they were.

As she started down toward the slough, she looked back over her shoulder at a call from the road, and waved to Lupe and her brother on their way to school. Each of them carried a tin lunch pail which caught the sun's rays and flashed brightly with every step they took. Evidently they had missed the school bus again. Time and the Romeros never seemed to be in agreement. Now they would be late to school, walking a mile with the sun on their backs.

It was easy to tell exactly where the slough began. For one thing, the greasewood growing around the edge of it was a deeper green and the bushes larger than those to be found in more arid sections. Furthermore, beyond the greasewood leaned the tules, their reedy stalks permanently bent by the blustering autumn winds. And only around water were tules to be found.

So as Janey came within sight of them, she stepped more cautiously and took greater care to keep the thick clumps of greasewood between her and the tules. In there, among the tules, was where the ducks would be.

Closer and closer she approached the slough. Now the

sandy soil was wet under her feet. It felt cold to her bare toes, but as it continued to get wetter and wetter, she was thankful she didn't have on shoes. She would only have had to take them off.

Suddenly, she froze in her tracks as motionless as a listening rabbit. A sound had come to her, the sound of ducks feeding happily, and quietly quacking their content. Janey dropped to her knees and crept forward, still keeping close to the greasewood, but careful not to brush against it lest its sudden motion frighten the birds. At last the still water of the slough was in sight. She could have reached out and touched the tules had she wished. And there before her delighted eyes were at least a dozen ducks. Some of them were paddling about smoothly, leaving a few quiet ripples behind them on the glassy surface of the water. Their sleek necks, arched tight against their gray-white breasts, changed from black to brilliant green as their iridescent feathers caught the sunlight. Others were diving into the water, their sharp tails and kicking red feet pointed absurdly straight up to the sky.

Janey sank back on her heels and looked happily around her. The greasewood was higher than her head, shutting off the horizon. But the ducks and tules were still there in plain sight, while above her, arching over it all and making everything vast and complete, was the cloudless sky. For the moment this was all the world there was, and it belonged exclusively to her, Janey Larkin. The ducks, the sunlight, even the farthest inch of sky was hers. Just the world and Janey Larkin. This was what it meant to inherit the earth, she thought, folding her hands contentedly in her lap and closing her eyes. She wanted to make sure the picture was hers for keeps. Yes, there it was behind her closed eyelids, every detail of it vivid and clear. And there she would hold it until another autumn gave it back to her living and real.

How long she had been crouching there Janey did not know, but all at once she had the distinct feeling that she was no longer alone. Cautiously she turned to look around and saw—Bounce Reyburn. He was sneaking toward the slough, a gun in his hands. Janey knew at once what he was there for and a wild, unreasoning rage took possession of her. He had come here to kill these birds that she loved, to shoot them as they swam and played about in the water. But he wouldn't shoot these. Not while she was here, at least, and could prevent it.

Still facing Bounce, Janey rose from behind the greasewood clumps and waved her arms. Behind her she could hear a rush of wings and the splash of water as the ducks rose out of the slough. At the same instant, Bounce raised his gun. But Janey stood between him and his target. During the moment that the gun was trained on her and Janey looked down its long blue barrel, it seemed to her to be as big as the cannons she had seen reposing tranquilly on the public lawns of the small towns she had come through. But she stood her ground fearlessly and defied Bounce, whose face was red with fury.

"What do you mean spoilin' my shot?" he demanded, striding toward her.

"I didn't want the ducks killed," said Janey simply.

"Oh, *you* didn't want them killed. Well, who are you?"

"I'm Janey Larkin."

Bounce looked closely at her. "You're that meddlin' kid that's always sneakin' around where you haven't any business bein'."

Janey said nothing.

"Well, let me tell you something," Bounce went on, dropping his voice now in that threatening way he had. "You keep out of my way from now on, you understand? And keep away from this slough. This isn't any place for you at all. I've told you before not to come snoopin' around this neck of the woods and I mean it. Now beat it."

So Janey, with one backward glance over her shoulder at the spot where the ducks had been, started away from Bounce and the slough, her heart now as filled with hate as a short time ago it had been filled with happiness. Funny how just one person could change everything, she thought as she trudged along. She had covered a third of the distance to the shack when she heard the muffled report of a shotgun. But Janey didn't look back. Only, her mouth set itself more grimly and her eyes, looking straight ahead of her, smoldered dangerously. It would have gone hard with Bounce if Janey could have got her hands on him at that moment!

She felt a little better that afternoon when Dad came home with the back end of the car filled to the top with eucalyptus wood. There were at least two more loads waiting to be hauled, so the Larkins wouldn't have to worry about fuel for some time to come. To Janey the wood pile was a very satisfying sight. It had a nice permanent look about it. Surely

they wouldn't go away while the wood pile lasted! Although the best of the cotton had by this time been picked, there was yet enough left in the fields to make it worth while for Mr. Larkin to stay. But more and more of the pickers were leaving and one day there were so few pupils at the camp school that Miss Peterson announced it would close the following week. The news came as a blow to Janey.

On the Friday which marked the last day of school, she lingered after the half-dozen other boys and girls had left.

"Where are you going now?" she asked Miss Peterson.

"I don't know for sure, Janey."

"Won't I ever see you again?" The thought had just occurred to her and she felt as if she simply couldn't let it happen. She couldn't just say: "Good-by" to Miss Peterson and let her walk right out of her life forever. Not Miss Peterson.

"That's hard to say, Janey. We might meet again some time. Probably you will be coming this way next year when the cotton is ready for picking, and if I don't get a regular school, I might be right here at Camp Miller waiting for one Janey Larkin to walk in and say 'Howdy.'"

Janey smiled at Miss Peterson, but not happily. She knew the teacher was merely trying to be kind and that in all probability they would never see each other again. More than ever Janey wished they didn't have to move on. They had been nearly three months in this place. That was long enough to make you feel as if you belonged. She had found friends here. They even had a wood pile now. It would be harder than ever to go when the time came, as it always did.

But already forces were at work to keep Janey in the San Joaquin Valley for longer than she guessed or could have dreamed.

With the coming of December, the sun suddenly vanished entirely and a heavy blanket of fog spread over the land. It blotted out the blue of the sky, merging the clouds into one thick gray mass. It seemed to rise up out of the ground as steam rises from a kettle, shrouding everything in mistiness and sliding ghost-like into houses whenever a door was opened. You could feel it like a fine rain on your face, and sometimes it was so thick Janey couldn't see Lupe's house just across the road. And it was while the fog held the land close-wrapped that Mom caught a severe cold.

It started innocently enough with a few sniffles and Mom's assurance that she'd be all right tomorrow. But when tomorrow came, she was far from all right, and each day she grew steadily worse. Then came the morning when she didn't bother to get up and Janey cooked breakfast for Dad.

That was the morning when whatever courage Janey might have possessed deserted her. Seeing Mom lying with closed eyes, her face pinched and drawn, a terrible thought had shaken Janey, leaving her weak and almost frantic. For the first time in her life she was afraid. Suppose Mom should die? She must be frightfully sick, sick enough to die, or she would never stay in bed abandoning Dad to a little girl's dubious care. Suppose suddenly there was no Mom to fuss over her and to love her; to walk with silent indifference through each day's happenings and then unexpectedly to say: "Rivers of water in a dry place"? What would happen to her and to Dad if anything should happen to Mom? Janey couldn't imagine life without her. It would be like meat without salt. An aching tightness gripped her throat and she was fighting against tears when Mrs. Romero knocked at the door.

One look at the sick woman and, "You should go to the hospital," she declared.

Mrs. Larkin wearily opened her eyes. "It takes money for that," she said, and began coughing again.

"Not at the county hospital; it doesn't cost anything," replied the patient, kindly Mrs. Romero.

"I know that. But we haven't lived in this county long enough to have the right to go there," said Mrs. Larkin.

The visitor nodded understandingly. "That's right," she said, "I had forgotten. But then you should call Dr. Peirce. He has an office right over here in the town and he'd come if you sent for him."

"It'd take money to pay him and we haven't any to spare," said Mrs. Larkin. "I'll be all right if I just keep in close for a few days."

But Mrs. Romero didn't look so sure of that as she went away, and Janey was far from sure, too. Unless they got a doctor, Mom would die. But if they couldn't pay him how could they ask him to come?

Suddenly an idea sprang at Janey and stopped her right in the middle of the room. The willow plate. Perhaps he would come for the willow plate. She glanced at Mom, who had drifted into a restless sleep. Quick as a wink, Janey pulled out the old suitcase and began digging into it. Out came the willow plate. Another look at Mom and she slipped into her warm new coat. Quietly she opened the door and the next minute was speeding across the road toward the Romeros'.

Mrs. Romero met her on the front steps, a sweater held around her shoulders. She had seen Janey coming.

"I'm going for the doctor," said Janey. "Will you take care of Mom until we get back?"

"Sure," said Mrs. Romero and waited only long enough to tell Janey where to find him before she started for the Larkin shack.

Up the road and through the fog went Janey, her arms clasped over the willow plate. She had about a mile to go along the same road that Lupe and her brother took to school. In spite of her worries, Janey couldn't resist playing she was on her way this very minute to a "regular" school where she belonged.

Her feet, clad now in canvas sneakers, twinkled with quick purpose, and before long the brick front of the school house loomed out of the fog before her. Here she turned to the right and followed along the street until she came to a large square building with stairs going up at one end. Janey climbed the stairs and at the top found herself in a long dark hall. Hesitantly she walked along, peering at every door until at the very end she came upon one that had the words, "C. E. Peirce, M.D. Enter," printed on it. Slowly Janey turned the door knob and went inside. This was the waiting room but there was nobody waiting in it. Janey had expected to find the doctor here and a pang of disappointment shot through her. But another door leading from this room into the next bore a sign announcing that "Doctor is in; please be seated." So Janey sat, still hugging the willow plate.

For a long time she sat and nothing happened. Not a sound did she hear and she was beginning to wonder what she should do next when she heard a chair creak in the next room. This was followed by the sound of someone moving about. Then the door was flung open and Dr. Peirce stood on the threshold. He saw Janey and gave a start of surprise.

"Good Lord!" he exclaimed. "How long have you been here?"

"A long time," said Janey, rising. Ten minutes can seem a very long time when you have a loved one at home who is terribly sick and when you are fighting with yourself not to be sorry because you are giving up a willow plate. Janey looked hard at the doctor. He was an elderly man, with heavy shoulders that had become bowed a little from the weight of other people's troubles. There was a fierce scowl between his eyes, and his voice was gruff. But there was that in his face which made Janey know at once that here was someone who would be kind and whom you didn't need ever to be afraid of.

"Well, who's sick?" asked the doctor, impatiently.

"My mother," Janey replied, "and she didn't want you to come and see her because we haven't much money left and the cotton is nearly all gone, but I brought you the willow plate."

Janey had spoken all in one rush because it was the hardest thing she had ever had to say and she wanted to get it over with as quickly as possible. Now she held the plate out to the doctor. But he wasn't even looking at it.

"How long has she been sick?" he asked.

"She's had a cold three days," said Janey, still holding out the plate.

"Good Lord!" It was a groan this time. "Pneumonia probably by now. Well, come along. Standing around here isn't doing her any good."

"But the plate," insisted Janey. "Don't you want it?"

"No," said the doctor, emphatically, "I do not."

He sounded angry, but Janey, crossing her arms over the plate and once more hugging it to her, noticed that his eyes looking deep into hers were still kind.

Together they went down the long hall and down the stairs and out into the fog to where the doctor's car was parked. It looked almost as old as the Larkins' only not quite so chewed up inside. And very soon they were back at the shack.

Janey was afraid Mom might be cross when she saw the doctor, but Mom was too sick to care. Gently and thoroughly he examined her, muttered: "Pneumonia," and began rummaging in his bag and giving Mrs. Romero and Janey directions in a rumbling voice.

At length he went away, promising to return the next morning. But the comfort of his presence stayed behind him in the shack, and Janey's heart was lighter than it had been for several days as she gratefully tucked the willow plate back into the suitcase.

8. MORE TROUBLE

DAD DIDN'T TRY TO GO TO WORK THE FOLLOWING DAY. MOM
was too sick. Nobody knew what might happen. Dr. Peirce
came and stayed half the forenoon and went away, saying he
would return that evening.

Before he left, Dad took some money out of the buckskin
bag and tried to give it to him. "Keep it for medicine," the
doctor said abruptly and walked out of the house as if he
were angry. But they all knew he wasn't. It was just his way.

And somehow it made it easier. Mrs. Romero hardly left the shack at all that day, but turning the baby, Betty, over to Janey, she devoted herself to Mrs. Larkin.

Because the shack was so small and because Betty was no quieter than most babies, Janey spent the greater part of the day at the Romero house, where Betty could laugh and holler to her heart's content without bothering anyone. Watching her, Janey almost envied Betty her lack of knowledge and understanding. Life must be very easy for a baby, especially one as spoiled as Betty. She had long since ceased to envy Lupe her little sister.

At half-past three, Lupe and Tony came home from school. Lupe's eyes when she saw Janey were round and solemn and deep with sympathy.

"How is your mother?" she asked.

"She was about the same when I went over a few minutes ago," Janey replied.

"Then she is no worse," said Lupe, and Janey felt strangely relieved, as if Lupe's statement had made Mom suddenly better. It was good to have friends like these who cared about what happened to you and tried to cheer you when you were sad. Now Lupe was chatting about school, but Janey wasn't paying much attention. Her mind was too full of things as she stood at the window, her eyes on the house across the road, the house which seemed at this moment to be holding all the trouble in the world. But all at once one word in Lupe's rambling recital caught Janey's attention, spinning her around.

"What did you say?" she demanded.

"I said we have a new teacher at our school. Her name is Miss Peterson."

"What does she look like?" It couldn't be *the* Miss Peterson, Janey assured herself even as she put the question.

"She's kind of fat and real nice. I like her," Lupe added judicially, pleased that she had at last succeeded in catching Janey's interest.

"Listen, Lupe. When you go to school tomorrow, you ask her if she was at Camp Miller school this fall. You won't forget, will you? I think she's the same teacher I had there."

"Sure, I'll ask her," promised Lupe.

Further talk between the two girls was interrupted by the arrival of Dr. Peirce. Janey ran across the road and reached the shack a few minutes after the doctor had gone inside. Quietly she edged open the door and slipped into the room. The doctor was bending over her mother. No one spoke. At last he took a thermometer out of Mrs. Larkin's mouth and moved over to the window with it.

"She's holding her own," he said to the thermometer. "Putting up a good fight. Her courage may pull her through."

Courage. The word recalled to Janey a forgotten conversation. Dad had talked about courage on that day when she had first gone to Camp Miller school. What had he said? "It takes courage to live the way we do without losing your grip on things." That was it. She had doubted Mom's courage on that far-away day. But now the doctor was saying that Mom did have courage. Janey didn't doubt any longer. As she looked toward the bed, she wondered how she could ever have doubted.

They didn't bother to go to bed that night, not really to bed. Dad made Janey lie down on the back seat cushion and she went to sleep with all her clothes on. In her dreams, Miss Peterson came to her with a bottle of medicine and told her to take three drops of it and then her mother could go to the district school with Lupe. It was such a funny dream, it made Janey smile in her sleep.

And the next morning her father was smiling, too.

"Your mother is better today," he said.

Janey jumped up and looked across the room. Mom was looking at her, and as Janey's eyes met hers, Mom put out her hand. With a bound Janey was beside the bed, holding onto that hand as if she never intended to let it go.

"You're going to get well, aren't you, Mom?" she cried.

"Certainly," was all Mom said, but it sounded very final.

And when a little later Dr. Peirce called, he said that Mom was over the worst of it and with proper care should be all right in a month's time.

Janey thought quickly. Then they couldn't go away for another month, no matter what happened. But the first week in December was nearly gone and next week they would owe another five dollars for the rent. There was still a little money left in the buckskin bag. Would it be enough? What would Dad find to do for another month, though? The cotton plants were just blackened sticks now and what cotton remained wasn't worth the picking. But certainly they couldn't go until Mom was better, much better.

That afternoon Dad hauled the second load of wood and worked at the wood pile until dark, cutting it up into stove lengths. It was hard work because eucalyptus wood is almost as tough as iron. Once while Mom was asleep, Janey went out to watch him. Her heart swelled with pride as she saw Dad bring the ax down in swift, sure strokes. Dad could do anything, she felt sure.

Some of Mr. Anderson's cattle stood at the fence watching too, their dark shapes blurred in the fog.

"I should think those cows would be cold." Janey snuggled deeper into her own warm coat as she spoke.

"They're used to it," said Mr. Larkin. He straightened up to look at the cattle. "They're in good shape," he added, swinging the ax again.

Janey giggled. "You couldn't really tell in this fog what they looked like," she said, teasingly.

Dad grinned. "That's enough of your impudence, young one. Haven't we been living next door to Anderson's stock for three months? I sized it up the first day we moved in here. It's second nature for an old stock man to do that."

Jancy lifted her head proudly at his words. "We had cows like that once, didn't we?"

"We sure did," answered her father. "And a few horses and a house."

He had stopped work again and was staring into the fog as if among its boiling motes he could see again that ranch in the Dust Bowl.

"And I was awful little and you used to hold me on the saddle in front of you." Janey was recalling a story she had heard many times, and loved.

"You were a cute little tyke then," said Mr. Larkin.

"But I'm not a cute little tyke now?" asked Janey anxiously.

"No," came the surprising and good-natured answer, "you stopped being that about five years back. But you're a pretty good girl now."

"Which way do you like me best?" Janey grinned.

"It's hard to say." Mr. Larkin reached for a length of wood and tweaked Janey's ear at the same time. "But I'm sure not going to like you at all if you don't get back into the house and see how your mother's doing. She's been alone all of ten minutes. Run along now."

So Janey, taking a few sticks of wood along with her, went back into the house, while the chop, chop of Dad's ax continued to sound behind her.

That evening with supper over and Mom made comfortable for the night, Dad and Janey were chatting quietly about this and that when heavy footsteps came bounding up the steps, and there was a sharp knock at the door.

Before Dad opened the door, Janey knew who would be there, for this was the middle of the month and the rent was due. So she was not surprised when Bounce Reyburn stalked into the room remarking that it was a "dirty night." To this, Janey silently and fervently agreed, but not for the reason Bounce meant.

He nodded toward the bed in the corner. "Sick?" he asked.

"Yes," said Mr. Larkin quietly. He did not ask Bounce to sit down.

"Tough," replied Bounce briefly, then: "Well, I guess you know why I'm here."

"Yes," said Mr. Larkin again, but not making any move to draw forth the buckskin bag.

"Well, let's have it." Bounce sounded impatient.

"Sorry, Reyburn"—Mr. Larkin's voice was still quiet, but steady, very steady—"I can't pay you anything this month. We would have been out of here this week if my wife hadn't got sick. She can't start traveling again for some time. Cotton picking is over and I don't know whether I'll be able to find any other work. I've got to keep what little I have left for food. As far as this shack is concerned, it isn't worth the rent you're asking, and if we moved out, nobody'd live in it again this winter, and you know it."

It was a long speech for Dad. Janey listened breathlessly, watching Bounce to see what his next move would be. In the glaring light of the gasoline lantern, she could see that ugly glint come into his eyes. He took a threatening step toward Dad.

Janey could feel her cheeks grow hot with sudden rage. Couldn't this man see that Mom was sick? Why couldn't he leave them alone? Why didn't Dad do something to get him out of here instead of just talking? Oh, if only she were in Dad's place! She'd show this Bounce Reyburn a thing or two! It was awful to stand here shaking with fury and helpless to do anything about it just because you were a little girl instead of a grown man.

"Listen, buddy, there's no use whinin' about your hard luck to me," Bounce was saying; "it's either pay up or get out. Savvy?"

"Well, get this and get it straight." There was an edge to

Dad's voice that Janey had never heard before. "I'm not paying up and I'm not moving out. And what would you like to
do about it?"

Bounce took another step toward Dad and this time Dad
stepped up to meet him. It was then Janey's heart began to
pound with pleasurable excitement. There was going to be
a fight, after all. She knew it. Dad would sock this Bounce,
sock him hard. It never occurred to her that Dad might get
socked too. Dad was invincible. Bounce wouldn't have a
chance. Oh, it would be good to witness the vanquishing of
this man whom she hated! This man who had called her a
thief and who had killed the ducks. It was fair enough, she
supposed, that he should charge them rent, since the house
didn't belong to them. But he richly deserved a good beating
for all the other things. And now Dad was about to take care
of that. It was a glorious moment.

But before a blow could be struck and to Janey's immense
disappointment, a cry from the sick bed halted hostilities
momentarily.

"Pay him and get rid of him," called Mom. "Fighting will
only get us all into trouble. He could have you arrested, Jim,
and then where would we be? You haven't got a chance."

"I won't pay him," said Dad sullenly, turning back to face
Bounce. "Right's right and wrong's wrong."

Janey looked at Bounce as she considered Mom's words.
There was no weakening in his face. It was as stubbornly
resolute as Dad's. And suddenly Janey was afraid. As eagerly
as she had desired conflict a moment ago, now she longed
to prevent it. Mom was right, as usual. They were the help-

less victims of this man. Even though Dad won in a fight between them, Bounce would be the final victor. Now, as the two men glared at each other, a terrible and nameless danger seemed to hover over the room, thickening with each passing second like an invisible fog.

They mustn't fight. Dad would go to jail if they did. Already Janey could see him behind prison bars. But Bounce wouldn't leave until the rent was paid; and Dad had refused to pay it. What could she do? What *could* she do? Suddenly, she rushed between the men, her arms extended as if to keep them apart.

"Wait!" she cried, lifting a tense face to her father. "Wait, I've thought of something."

The men, taken by surprise, relaxed their taut figures a little, while their angry eyes fastened on Janey's quick figure. They saw her dart to the bed and haul from under it the old suitcase. For a moment, her hands fumbled in its depths, and then she whirled about. In her hands was the willow plate.

"Here," she said, holding it out to Bounce. "We'll pay the rent with this."

A cry of protest came from Mom but no one paid any attention to her.

Bounce flicked the plate with disdainful eyes. "What do I want with somebody's old dish?" he asked.

"It's so pretty," said Janey, her voice shaking a little. "It must be worth five dollars." But in her heart she doubted it. Five dollars seemed an enormous sum for one plate. So she added shrewdly: "Besides, it's the only thing we have left."

She judged Bounce mean enough to have this last seem more important to him than the plate's possible value.

Bounce took the plate and flipped it over carelessly while Janey's heart skipped a beat.

"You set quite a store by this, don't you?" he observed.

Janey nodded hopefully and watched his face as Bounce brooded over the thing in his hands. An idea was slowly taking form in his dull brain. But Janey never could have guessed what he was thinking, which was simply this:

Bounce Reyburn knew the Larkins held receipts for every payment of rent they had made. He knew, too, that not one dollar of that money had ever found its way to Mr. Anderson in whose name it had been collected, that he was completely ignorant of Bounce's business dealings with this family. Now Bounce held in his hands the one treasure they possessed. Perhaps if he kept it a while, long enough to make them feel its loss, they would be willing, when he should make the offer, to trade the tell-tale receipts for the willow plate. Then he could send them on their way and nobody, least of all Mr. Anderson, would be the wiser.

The longer Bounce mulled over this scheme, the more it appealed to him. Those receipts had worried him right along. If they should ever find their way to his employer, Bounce knew he would be in serious trouble.

He glanced up at last to Mr. Larkin. "O.K. It's a deal."

So signing a receipt for the willow plate, Bounce finally disappeared with it into the night and the fog.

Janey stood staring helplessly at the closed door. It was gone. The only beautiful thing they owned. The thing that

for Janey had had the power to make drab things beautiful
and to a life of dreary emptiness bring a sense of wonder and
delight. She felt as if her heart had been plucked from her.
Now she knew how Dad had felt when he had lost the ranch
in Texas. Now she knew what he had meant that day he had
said it took courage not to lose your grip on things. She didn't
have to wait, after all, until she was grown up to learn that
there are at least two kinds of courage in the world. Well, she
wasn't going to lose her grip, either. She swallowed the ache
in her throat and went to Mom, who was calling her.

"That was a brave thing you did," said Mom. "You
shouldn't have had to do it."

"It was just an old plate," Janey said consolingly, but feeling as if she had slandered an old friend.

However, Mom wasn't fooled.

"I know what it meant to you." Her hand closed comfort-
ingly over Janey's. "I've known all the time. It was your
mother's. You shouldn't have had to give it up."

Janey turned to her in astonishment. So that was why Mom
had always protected the plate! That was why she had never
let it be used! Mom knew what it had stood for. Perhaps she
had loved it as Janey did! Maybe even more, since she was a
grown-up and must therefore have a greater capacity for
loving. Janey clung quietly to Mom's hand while something
like peace crept closely about her heart. Somehow, in spite
of the aching misery of its loss, it was almost worth the
sacrifice to have discovered how Mom felt about the willow
plate.

9. *THE WILLOW PLATE*

THE NEXT TWO DAYS WERE QUITE UNEVENTFUL. MOM CON-
tinued to improve, Dad tried to find work, and Janey managed to take care of Mom and to keep house with the neighborly help of Mrs. Romero. It was good to be busy, so busy
that at times she could almost forget about the willow plate.
Almost, but never entirely. There was some small comfort in
knowing that at last it had found a decent home. For of
course Janey believed that Bounce had turned it over to Mr.
Anderson, in whose name he had taken it.

On the third day, Miss Peterson came to call. The teacher

142

at Lupe's school had turned out to be *the* Miss Peterson. Janey, answering the knock on the door and expecting to find one of the Romeros on the top step, was completely unprepared for the splendid surprise. For a moment she stood foolishly, unable to say a word.

"Howdy, Janey, won't you let me in?" Miss Peterson greeted her.

Janey flung the door wide and although a large slice of fog came in with the visitor, it seemed as if by some magic it had turned to pure sunshine. Miss Peterson could make everything different. Her arms were full of paper bags that bulged in an interesting way, and her face wore a broad smile.

"I would have come yesterday if I hadn't had to make a trip into Fresno. But I brought a few peace offerings with me."

Miss Peterson was putting the bundles on the table as she spoke and Janey, still rather dazed and trying to be helpful, proved so awkward that one of the bags upset, spilling sunshine in the form of oranges all over the room. In the scramble to pick them up, Miss Peterson managed to get acquainted with Mrs. Larkin and to put Janey at her ease.

It was rather late in the afternoon. Miss Peterson had had to wait until school was out before making her visit, so she hadn't been in the shack very long before Mr. Larkin came home. The minute he walked into the room, Janey knew something was troubling him, and something more than ordinarily disturbing. It would have to be pretty bad to make Dad look as sadly discouraged as he did now. It didn't take her long to decide what that something was. The work was gone. They would have to move. And there wasn't anything she could do about it, not anything at all. Not even the fact that Mom wouldn't be strong enough to travel for a long time could make any difference. They would have to go anyway.

Dad tried to throw off his gloom as he greeted Miss Peterson and thanked her for her gifts. But his smile was not very convincing and his attempts at conversation even less so. After a few moments, Miss Peterson rose and went over to the bed.

"As soon as you are able to spare her, I want Janey to come to school," she told Mrs. Larkin.

Janey, hearing the words that once would have meant so much to her, was surprised to find that now they had no meaning whatsoever except to mock this moment. She found herself wishing they might have been left unsaid. But, of course, Miss Peterson had spoken them sincerely. She couldn't possibly know what Janey knew. And suddenly, looking at Miss Peterson, so friendly and so kind, and still thinking of what she had said, Janey didn't regret those words, after all. They made her feel somehow on the edge of belonging and a little closer to Lupe and the willow plate.

Dad moved over to the window and spoke without turning round.

"There's no use her starting school now," he said. "As soon as my wife is able to travel, and maybe before that, we'll be leaving. There's no more work around here and we've got to be heading toward the Imperial if we don't want to lose out all around."

"I understand," was all Miss Peterson said as she reached for her coat. At the door, she paused to give Janey a hug. "I'll see you again soon," she promised.

And she did. It was on Christmas Day, and again her arms were full of bundles. Janey hadn't thought much about its being Christmas. Mom was getting a little stronger every day, and of course Janey was glad of that, but she knew all the time that when Mom was able to leave her bed, they would load up the car and be on their way. Dr. Peirce had said they must wait a month, but Dad couldn't wait that long. They would have to chance it, taking the best care of Mom they could. The money in the buckskin bag was running low, and they must move on while there was still enough left to buy gasoline and the things they would need before Dad found work again. So Janey knew that this visit of Miss Peterson's would be the last time they would see each other, most likely. Miss Peterson knew it too. And though she and Janey tried to be gay and to make believe they would meet again next summer, they each knew it was really good-by. So it wasn't a very merry Christmas in spite of the bundles.

At last one day Dad announced quietly: "We'll be on our way tomorrow."

They were finally spoken, the words Janey for three long months had been dreading to hear. Tomorrow they were going away from the Romeros, away from Miss Peterson and the "regular" school, and away from the willow plate. Never before had Janey left so much behind her. Never again would she want so much to stay.

On that last afternoon, with everything packed and ready

to put into the car, Janey came to a sudden decision. She couldn't leave without one more look at the willow plate. It just wasn't possible to go away, perhaps forever, without telling the willow plate good-by.

Neither Mom nor Dad paid any attention to her when she put on her blue coat and slipped outdoors. Probably they thought she was going over for a last visit with Lupe. Janey was thankful that they asked no questions.

It was cold, bitterly cold. The fog lay close about her, collecting in tiny beads on the rough surface of her coat. She couldn't see more than fifty yards ahead of her, but she followed along by the barbed-wire fence in the direction of the Anderson place. When she came to the slough she skirted it and headed north, hoping to come upon the little road she had seen leading away from the old wooden bridge that day of her first visit. After much walking she came upon it. Turning to the right, she kept to the road until she came at last to the bridge. Here she paused for a moment to look back along the river. How changed everything was! The willows were no longer leafy and frond-like. Their bare branches were mere lines etched in criss-cross patterns against the fog. The water was as silent as before, but gray and cold and uninviting. Janey shivered and hurried on.

The ranch house was unchanged, however. It looked as weatherbeaten and friendly as ever. Danger, the dog, was nowhere in sight.

Straight up to the front steps Janey went, and knocked on the door. In just a moment it was opened and an astonished woman asked Janey what she wanted.

"I want to talk to Mr. Anderson, please," Janey answered.

"Won't you come in?" The woman, who Janey guessed must be Mrs. Anderson, stepped aside, and her small visitor walked resolutely in.

Janey found herself in a large room with chairs scattered about it in welcoming positions, their outstretched arms inviting her to be comfortable. One of them had been turned completely around to face the hearth, where a fire danced brightly. She could see the top of a man's head above the chair back, and she hoped this would turn out to be Mr. Anderson. It did. As soon as the woman said: "Someone to see you, Nils," the head moved, a tall body rose out of the chair, and Mr. Anderson turned to face his caller.

"Hello," he said at sight of Janey. "Won't you sit down and tell me what I can do for you?"

Janey backed over to a chair and settled herself gingerly on the very edge of it. Her resoluteness seemed to have deserted her. Now that she was actually inside the Anderson house, the strangeness of her mission suddenly dawned upon her. What would Mr. Anderson think of her wanting to see the willow plate again? It was no longer any concern of hers. It belonged to him now. He might even be angry at this intrusion. She was a little uneasy as she began to speak.

"I guess you don't remember me," she faltered. "I'm Janey Larkin and once I came here to this place and Bounce and I quarreled and you came along and said I could have a dozen eggs."

All at once the politely inquiring look vanished from Mr. Anderson's face and a smile of remembering lit it up. "Of course. This is the little girl I was telling you about," he said, turning to his wife. "This is Mrs. Anderson, Janey."

"Pleased to meet you," said Janey, and ducked her head.

"You and Bounce haven't had more difficulty, have you, Janey?" Mr. Anderson chuckled good-humoredly.

Janey shook her head. "I've come to tell the willow plate good-by. We're going away tomorrow and I couldn't bear to go without seeing it once more."

Mr. Anderson looked puzzled. "The willow plate?" he asked vaguely. "What willow plate?" He glanced questioningly at his wife, but Janey saw that she was as puzzled as he, and cold fear gripped her heart. Surely they weren't going to let on they didn't know about the plate!

"Yes," pursued Janey, resolute once more, "don't you remember I told you about it that day I was here? And Bounce took it a while ago for the rent."

"Bounce!" Mr. Anderson fairly barked the name and Janey jumped so she nearly fell off the edge of her chair. "What's Bounce got to do with all this?"

"Why," exclaimed Janey, wonderingly, "Bounce is the one who collects your rent for you! We didn't have the money last time, so we gave him the willow plate instead."

Mr. and Mrs. Anderson's eyes met over Janey's head. The air seemed to be full of question marks. Mr. Anderson's face was suddenly so full of anger that Janey rose. Evidently they didn't want her to see the willow plate, after all. But the man put out a hand. "Sit down," he said, kindly. "Suppose you tell me the whole story from the very beginning. I want all of it."

Deciding she had nothing to fear and glad that at last she could put her trust in this man just as she had wanted to do that day under the willows, Janey once more perched herself on the edge of her chair and began her story. She told it straightforwardly and simply without any emphasis on any particular part. Except when Dad won second prize in the contest and then a note of pride did creep into her voice.

"We got this coat with some of the money," she said in an aside to Mrs. Anderson.

"And a very pretty one it is," was her reply.

They exchanged knowing smiles with each other, quite ignoring Mr. Anderson, since no man could be expected to appreciate a thing like that.

"Why didn't you come to me before?" Mr. Anderson asked when Janey had finished.

"There was no reason to come," said Janey. "I wouldn't be here now if I hadn't wanted to see the willow plate once more."

"Well, you see, Janey, I didn't know anything about the rent. Whatever money Bounce got from you, he kept. I have never seen the willow plate." Mr. Anderson paused for a moment, frowning at the floor. "But I intend to see it very soon," he added in a tone which Janey was certain boded no good for Bounce Reyburn.

But in the meantime where was the willow plate? All this talk about the Larkins and about Bounce and his dishonesty only mildly interested Janey. She had come to see the plate.

"I think the plate will have to wait a little while," Mr. Anderson replied to her question. "I want to talk to your father before I talk to Bounce." He rose and stood looking down at the small girl. "It wouldn't surprise me a bit, Janey, if you didn't pull out of here tomorrow."

"Honest?" cried Janey, jumping to her feet, her blue eyes dancing.

Mr. Anderson chuckled quietly. "You're a funny little coot," was all he said, but Janey liked the way he said it.

Janey hadn't noticed when Mrs. Anderson left the room, but now she appeared wearing a hat and coat.

"I'm going with you to the Larkins', Nils," she said.

"Good," replied her husband, heartily. "I'll get the car."

Janey never forgot that ride back to the shack. She sat between Mr. and Mrs. Anderson. They hardly spoke, but the air was full of suspense, a nice kind of suspense holding the promise that everything was going to be all right. Janey could feel the sympathy of these two grown-ups. She even stopped worrying about the willow plate. She knew the Andersons would see that she got it again. She hoped Dad wouldn't be cross with her for going to the Anderson ranch alone. She supposed she should have asked leave to go, but suppose he had refused to allow her? Suppose they had just gone away tomorrow without ever saying a word to Mr. Anderson? They would have lost the willow plate forever. Janey shuddered at the thought, and Mrs. Anderson tucked the lap robe closer around her, thinking she was cold.

"Anyway," thought Janey, "it will be worth a scolding, a good hard one, to have the willow plate back."

But Janey didn't get a scolding, not that evening anyway. For with Nils Anderson's visit to the shack, the lives and fortunes of the Larkins were changed. Never again would they be wanderers upon the earth, never again would Janey long in vain to go to a "regular" school. Mr. Anderson was shown the receipts which Bounce had signed and which were positive proof of his dishonesty. Long and earnestly the two men talked while the women and Janey listened. Darkness settled down over the land, and Mr. Larkin rose and lit the gasoline lantern and the talking continued. Much of it was about the ranch in the Dust Bowl and about their lives before the drought forced the Larkins to leave Texas.

Mr. Anderson listened intently, interrupting only when Janey's father had reached the place in his story where the Larkins had taken refuge in the shack.

"I guess we shouldn't have done that, but you forget about such fine points when you live as we do," Mr. Larkin said.

The other man gestured impatiently. "Of course you should have done it. You're not the first family to occupy this shack. It has no value except to people like you, and anyone has been welcome to use it who wanted to. As far as that goes, I knew somebody was in it this fall, because I had seen you around here when I came over this way, and I had no objections to your staying. Of course I'd no idea of what Bounce was up to. He's probably been grafting on everyone who moved in here."

Mr. Anderson's face was set in hard, bitter lines. Janey couldn't help wishing Bounce would walk in now. It would be entirely different from that other night when he had been so sure of himself, and Dad had seemed at his mercy.

"Well, that's about all the story," Dad said after an interval of silence, rubbing his palms together in a slow, uncertain way.

Following his words, the silence continued, broken only by the rasping sound of his callused palms.

Everyone else sat motionless. Once the fire snapped loudly and out in the field a cow bawled. Janey, sitting cross-legged in the middle of the floor, looked anxiously from one face to another. Her father and mother were sitting on the edge of the bed, their eyes staring unseeingly before them. Plainly, Dad was talked out. It would be up to Mr. Anderson now.

Janey saw him exchange a look with his wife. Mrs. Anderson's head nodded slowly. With sudden decision, Mr. Anderson got to his feet.

"I'm letting Bounce go tomorrow, Larkin. I'll need a man in his place. The job is yours if you want it. Seventy-five dollars a month, a house, and all the eggs and milk you can use."

Mr. Larkin lifted his head and looked at Mr. Anderson in a dazed way. The offer was repeated. Slowly, awkwardly, Mr. Larkin got to his feet and put out his hand. He didn't say a word, and Janey was terrified for fear Mr. Anderson would think Dad didn't want the job. She wanted to scream to her father to say something, quick, before it should be too late. But Janey had learned during her strange life that there are times when only men are important, when even grown-up women don't matter at all. And certainly not little girls. This was distinctly one of those times. So she held her tongue and waited in an agony of suspense for whatever might happen.

It was with infinite relief that she saw Mr. Anderson grasp her father's hand, heard him say in friendly tones: "Take it easy there, Larkin. You deserve a break and I'm glad I can give it to you. I'll expect you to move in tomorrow."

There were almost no other words spoken, for the simple reason that there was nothing more anyone could say. Besides, this thing which had just happened to them struck the Larkins' hearts too deeply for chatter. They were unequal, even, to the obvious necessity of expressing gratitude. But, happily, it wasn't expected of them. The Andersons hastily said good-night and went away.

After they had gone, Mom spoke at last, looking squarely at Dad. "What he said was the truth. You do deserve a break. I'm glad it's come."

Dad reached out and drew Janey down on his knee, holding her close.

"I guess we have Janey to thank for it," he said.

Mom studied the two of them for a moment, then shook her head. "We should give thanks to that Power which is greater than Janey, greater than all of us."

Dad didn't reply, and Janey wondered as she felt his cheek against her head whether Mom meant God or the willow plate. Just to be safe, she offered up a silent prayer to both.

10. *"AS LONG AS WE WANT TO"*

LOADING THE CAR NEXT DAY WAS SHEER FUN. IT WAS THE FIRST time Janey could remember when it ever had been fun. How different was this moving from all the others! Yesterday morning she had been filled with sadness because they were going to leave the shack, and now here they were about to depart and she was as skippy as a grasshopper.

Before the arrival of the school bus, Janey ran across the road to Lupe. All the Romeros were jubilant over the Larkins' change of fortune, most of all Lupe.

"Now you can go to my school!" she cried happily, hugging Janey in a rare outburst of enthusiasm. "You will be in my class because we are the same age, and Miss Peterson will be your teacher again."

"Yes," Janey answered, "and we can ride together in the bus. I'll get picked up first because I will be farther from town than you."

But Lupe shook her head. "No," she said, "we will not ride together in the bus."

"But why not?" demanded Janey. "You aren't planning to miss it every day, are you?"

Lupe giggled. This Janey could be so funny.

"We are moving into town," Lupe explained. "My mother is going to start an eating place with enchiladas the way she knows how to make them. We will live back of the place. There's a garden with trees and in the summer I can help wait on the tables."

Janey was astonished, but relieved at the news. She had hated to leave Lupe and her family alone. It added to her own happiness to learn that good luck had come to the Romeros, too. But why hadn't Lupe told her before?

Lupe hung her head at the question and looked as if she had been found guilty of a great crime.

"I don't know," she said miserably, then added: "You were too sad."

It all sounded very mixed up, but Janey thought she understood. In the midst of Janey's trouble, Lupe had wanted to spare her friend her own good news lest by contrast it should add to Janey's misery. It was wonderful how Lupe could put herself in somebody else's place. Something told Janey that she would always be lucky with a friend like Lupe.

"Well, anyway," said Janey, her voice exaggeratedly matter-of-fact, "we'll be seeing each other at school, and you can visit me week-ends, and I can visit you. Perhaps we can both help with the enchiladas. Oh, I'm so glad we're not going away."

And to show how glad she was, Janey seized Lupe and spun her around until her black braids stood straight out from the sides of her head.

A few moments later, Janey was in the car, peering out of the back seat window for a farewell glimpse of the shack. It looked lonely and forlorn with the fog dripping off its eaves. Janey wondered if some day another family would find shelter under its roof. If that did happen, she hoped the new family would find as much happiness there as they had. But then, of course, the newcomers probably wouldn't possess a willow plate!

The house into which the Larkins were going to move was not, properly speaking, a house at all. It was a tank-house. On the ground floor was a fairly large room which served as a combination kitchen and living-room. Upstairs was a bedroom, and up above that was the huge tank containing the water supply for the ranch people.

Bounce had lived here until this day. But now he was gone. Before the arrival of the Larkins, Mr. Anderson had paid him and let him go. So Janey would never have to look into his shifty eyes again.

Mr. Anderson was on hand to greet them when the Larkins

drove in. There was a question trembling on Janey's lips when she caught sight of him. Dared she ask him now? As if he knew what was in her mind, "There's something waiting for you in there," he said with a nod toward the tank-house.

Janey ran across the yard, Danger bounding and barking at her heels. She hardly dared open the door. Suppose it wasn't what she thought? Slowly she turned the knob and walked in. At one side of the room was a square table pushed close against the wall. And reposing safely on it was the willow plate. Janey drew in her breath sharply, and for a second or two her knees felt too weak to hold her up. She hadn't realized until now how much she had feared for the plate. But here it was and none the worse for Bounce's brief ownership of it, she discovered as she picked it up.

She ran her fingers lovingly over its smooth surface and laid it against her cheek, delighting in the cool and certain feel of it.

"I'm never going to let you go again. Never," she promised in a whisper.

Dad and Mom soon joined her. Dad laid three five-dollar bills on the table.

"Where did they come from?" asked Janey in astonishment.

"They're what Bounce collected from us for rent. Mr. Anderson held them out of his wages when he settled up with him."

"Now we can pay Dr. Peirce," said Mom with pride in her voice. "I guess he can use the money to good purpose. And we won't be beholden to him any longer."

They let Mom do very little toward settling. She was still far from strong and Dad and Janey were equal to the task. There was an adequate amount of furniture in the two rooms, including two rocking chairs. Mom sat in one of them and gave orders. In just a twinkling, Dad had a fire roaring in the cook stove. Mrs. Anderson appeared with extra quilts. A lounge in the corner was to be Janey's bed. Never again would she sleep on the back seat cushion. Janey worked with a will, but had to stop every so often to try to grasp fully that they were really and truly settling down on the Anderson ranch to stay. It was all too wonderful to seem real.

When at last the place was as clean as Dad and Janey could make it—Bounce had been a careless housekeeper—and all the Larkin belongings with the exception of the willow plate had been tucked away, Janey turned to Mom.

"Now can we put the willow plate out where we can always see it?"

But Mom shook her head. "This isn't a proper house," she said, "it's only a tank-house even if it is comfortable. That plate came out of a real house and it's never going to be set out in anything except a real house."

So Janey put the willow plate out of sight in a bureau drawer where she could get at it easily. She couldn't help feeling a twinge of regret, though. The willow plate would have made a big difference in that room.

By the middle of January, the Larkins had settled into their new way of life and no family in the San Joaquin Valley was happier. Janey went to the district school, catching the bus at the end of the Anderson driveway every morning.

The weeks had made a difference in her appearance, for "all the milk and eggs you can use" will do a lot in a short time to make a skinny little girl begin to look well fed and healthy. And Janey had some new dresses that covered her knees, and shoes and stockings. It would have been hard to discover in the Janey who stood at the edge of the highway with her lunch pail in her hand awaiting the bus that thin and disheartened little girl sitting on the top step of the shack on a hot morning last September.

Mom was different too. The tired look had gone from her face, and she smiled readily these days. Dad was the same happy-go-lucky Dad, but there was a new set to his shoulders, and his voice when speaking of ranch matters had a confident ring that Janey hadn't heard since she was a tiny girl in Texas.

One day Janey, scouting around the dooryard, found some China lilies blooming behind a screen of genista. Dropping to her knees, she brushed her cheek against their brittle petals and was rewarded by a fragrance which held the authentic odor of spring. Beyond the fact that the fog had gone, she had been too taken up with her own affairs to notice that winter was passing.

But spring was on its way, there could be no doubt about it. At the river's edge, pussywillows were creeping along their stems, and the water was rising as the warm sun melted the snows of the Sierra Nevada Mountains away to the east. However, though spring was coming, it didn't arrive with a rush. There were many weeks after that first discovery of the China lilies when winds blustered around the tank-house, moaning drearily, and the rain fell in what seemed never-ending torrents.

Gradually, though, as the days lengthened, the sun seemed to get the better of winter. The clouds, broken up into billowy and unthreatening masses, rolled away, and spring settled as lightly as thistledown over the land. The willows and poplars began to look dusted with green, and from his perch atop the barn the first mockingbird of the season began practicing his favorite selections.

About this time Lupe announced to Janey at school one day: "I know a secret and it's about something you wished for once."

"What is it?" Janey asked immediately.

"I can't tell because it's a secret, but you'll like it when you know."

"When will I know?"

"Pretty soon," said Lupe, and Janey had to be satisfied with that. Lupe wouldn't respond to further questioning, but rolled her eyes mysteriously and seemed to relish hugely Janey's insistent curiosity.

"I think you're mean," Janey said at last with a pout.

But Lupe only giggled.

"Besides," Janey continued, confidentially, her pout gone, "there isn't anything I want now, Lupe. If you could hand me the whole world, there wouldn't be a thing in it I want that I haven't already got."

Lupe seemed unimpressed by this sweeping statement. She smiled teasingly. "You wait and see," she said.

So, in a way, Janey was a little prepared when one Saturday Manuel and six other Mexicans drove into the yard of the Anderson ranch. She had a feeling the instant she saw them that they had something to do with the secret. Wasn't Manuel Lupe's father? The very way in which he backed the truck around and parked it well out of the way proved beyond any doubt that this was no accidental happening. While Janey was turning it all over in her mind, Mr. Anderson appeared and walked across the yard with Manuel to where a big willow stood. There the two talked for a moment, while the other men lifted wooden forms out of the truck and carried them over to the willow. One man disappeared into the barn and after a little while emerged with a huge burlap bundle of straw on his back.

When Mr. Anderson left, Janey walked over to Manuel.

"What are you going to do?" she asked.

"We're starting to build a house, an adobe house," he answered. "It will be cool in summer, warm in winter, and it will last for anyway two hundred years. Will that be long enough, do you think?"

But Janey had only listened to the first of what he said. An amazing suspicion was taking form in her mind. She was remembering that day at the cotton picking contest when she had described her dream house to Lupe. Could this be the secret Lupe had meant? Suddenly, she knew it was. She looked around for Mr. Anderson. He was standing with Dad beside the barn. They were looking at a piece of paper. Janey ran to them.

"Who's going to live in the new house?" she asked, too excited to notice she was interrupting.

The two men exchanged knowing smiles, then Mr. Anderson said with tantalizing slowness: "Why, I kind of hoped you would, Janey. Here's the plan. How do you think you'll like it?"

Janey took a quick look at the paper, just enough of a look to discover that the house was to have four rooms and a bath. Having made sure of this, she turned and ran to the old wooden bridge. Standing in the middle of it, she glanced over to where Manuel and his men were working under the willow. Yes, it would be like the willow plate, all right. A bridge, a house, a willow tree. And three people, too. Dad and Mom and Janey. For a little longer she stood on the bridge, motionless. Then she whirled herself around three times in an excess of joyousness, and darted away to the tank-house, to share the good news with Mom and the willow plate. There wasn't in all the world at that moment a happier person than Janey Larkin.

As if the house weren't enough excitement for one season, a few days later Janey came home from school with the announcement that Miss Peterson had chosen her to be one of the girls in the May Day dance at Weston. This festival, celebrated on the big lawn of the Weston Union High School, was an annual event of great importance. People came from miles around to see it. Each season twelve district schools were named to take part, each one to have its own May Pole. This year Janey's school was one of them, and Janey herself was to be a dancer. Lupe was going to dance, too.

Faithfully, day by day, Janey practiced her steps, while equally faithfully Manuel and his men mixed mud and straw and pressed it into the wooden forms until row upon row of adobe bricks stood drying in the sun. At last the actual building of the house began. The walls went up, brick upon brick. It was a low and spreading house, looking as if it had grown out of the land it stood on, which indeed it had. Janey liked the fact that their house was being built out of the very soil of this ranch. It made it seem more than ever their own. Actually, of course, it belonged to Mr. Anderson, but they would live in it. Perhaps for as long as they wanted to. Would Mr. Anderson say that, if she asked him? Would she have the courage ever to put the question? She stopped in the middle of her dance to think this over. Perhaps it would be better just to go on as they were, feeling sure that all was well and not worrying about the future. After all, hadn't Mr. Anderson said he hoped she would live in the house? Of course he wanted them to stay. Janey went on with her dancing.

May Day came at last. It was the kind of day Janey would have ordered if Aladdin's genie had appeared before her and said: "You can have any kind of May Day you want." There was about it a kind of magic, for one breath of that morning was enough to make you forget winter as if it had never been. The sky was blue, as blue as Janey's eyes, as blue as the willow plate, as blue as the bowl of heaven should be on a day in spring before the sun of summer has had a chance to fade it.

Janey could hardly wait to get into her dress. It was the color of sunlight and it had ruffles over the shoulders and a wide sash. It was the first fluffy dress Janey had ever owned

and she was certain it was the loveliest one of its kind anywhere on land or sea.

A large crowd had already gathered when the Larkins
reached Weston. It enclosed the huge semicircular lawn in
front of the high school, men and women, girls and boys.
There were people with cameras maneuvering to get a view
that would include the twelve tall poles each topped by a
basket of flowers and draped with varicolored streamers.
These were the May Poles around which Janey and her com-
rades would be dancing.

The festival was to open with a parade of all the dancers
marching by twos around the edge of the lawn in front of the
crowd. The girls looked very festive in their brand-new fluffy
dresses. Janey and Lupe both wore yellow because their pole
was draped in yellow. Everyone was dressed from top to toe
in the color of her pole. Hair ribbon, dress, and socks all
were the same. Only the shoes were different. They were not
new, and some were a scuffed black and some were a scuffed
brown. And a lot of them were too large for their wearers.

After the parade, they all sang "The Star-Spangled Ban-
ner." Janey was proud to see that Dad took off his hat. She
lifted her eyes to the flag. Over and above them all, with
languid grace, it unfolded its vivid bars. There wasn't much
wind and sometimes it drooped almost against the pole. But
just when Janey had decided it might become entirely limp,
a fresh gust would seize it and lift it out over the crowd
again. It didn't matter in the least, she thought, as with eyes
glued to it she reached for the high notes in the national
anthem; it didn't matter in the least whether it floated from

the unpainted pole at Camp Miller or here above the tall gables of Weston Union High School. It was simply the flag; nothing could add to its splendor or dim its glory. She could feel that it stood for something important and big. But what that something was, she couldn't have said if anyone had asked her. It would take a grown-up to do that. For to Janey and to the other boys and girls standing there, the flag stood for their trust in the present and their hope in the future.

Next, the May Queen was crowned, and then Janey and Lupe with the others took their stations around their poles. But just before the music was to start, Janey saw Miss Peterson coming toward them. There was a teacher going to every pole. What could the matter be?

"Take your shoes off," said Miss Peterson, "and run quickly to the edge of the lawn with them."

In another instant the crowd was treated to the interesting sight of gaily colored dancers dashing toward them, their shoes held in their hands. And now everyone was the same color from top to toe. Even if some shoes were scuffed and too big it wouldn't make any difference.

Back went the dancers to the poles, and how they skipped and bounded in their stockinged feet! The turf felt like springs under them, and their feet were suddenly as light as feathers.

All at once the music blared forth, and the dancing began. Janey danced as she never had in all her hours of practicing. But, then, she had never danced in stockinged feet before. She lifted her knees high and never missed a beat of the music. At last came the moment for which everyone had been waiting. On a certain chord, the dancers ran up to their poles, seized a streamer, and backed away with it. Instantly all twelve May Poles became huge mushrooms of color spreading over the lawn. Then the weaving began. And suddenly Janey had an idea. She would dance each time around the pole for someone who had made this day possible for her. The May Pole dance would be her own private festival in celebration of their staying in this place.

"The first time is for Mom," thought Janey, lifting her knees higher than before. "The next one is Dad's."

Around and around the pole went Janey and the color traveled down its length with lightning speed. At last there was just one more circle to go and there was no one left to dance it for. Yes, there was. Janey almost missed a step as the thought struck her. Bounce Reyburn. If it hadn't been for his very meanness she might never have been here now. So Janey danced once for Bounce, wondering as she did so why people like him had to clutter up an otherwise satisfactory world. Was it because there had to be some bad mixed with the good to keep everything from becoming so sweet you couldn't stand it? Janey had the feeling, as the dance came to an end, that she would never really know the answer, not even when she finally became a grown-up.

Lupe was to return to the ranch with the Larkins to spend the night, and to inspect the new house. It was finished now. Only the furniture needed to be moved in. It was to be new furniture from Fresno, and ever since Janey had learned this she had felt as if she couldn't manage to exist until it came.

She might not have managed it, either, but for the excitement of the May Day festival.

Janey didn't wait for anything when they reached home, but insisted that Lupe come at once to see the new house. Lupe needed no urging. Up to the front door went Janey, too intent upon her own business to notice Mr. and Mrs. Anderson, who had come out of their own house at the Larkins' return and were now crossing the yard.

Janey put her hand on the new door knob and opened the door. She started into the house then stopped suddenly on the threshold, too stunned to move. The furniture had arrived! While she was celebrating the May, the van had come from Fresno and now there was a rug on the floor, she could feel it under her feet. She was vaguely aware of chairs standing about and a table or two. But the thing that held her spellbound was the fireplace. For on the mantelpiece above it, safely secured in its very center, was the willow plate. While she gazed upon it, its outlines became suddenly blurred and its pattern wavered. For the first time almost since Janey could remember, two tears ran down her cheeks. The willow plate had found a decent home at last.

She didn't go on into the house. There was something she had to know first. It wouldn't wait another instant. Janey turned and saw Mr. Anderson smiling at her. She tried to speak, failed, and tried again. "How long can we stay?" she asked him.

"As long as you want to, Janey," he said, his eyes as serious as Janey's own.

She swung around to Lupe. "Ask me how long we can stay," she demanded, fiercely.

"He just told you," said Lupe, nodding toward Mr. Anderson.

"That doesn't make any difference. Ask me. I want you to."

So Lupe, looking around at the grown-ups and feeling a little silly, said to Janey standing tense and eager before her: "How long are you going to stay?" just as she had asked at their first meeting in September.

Janey flung up her head, a look of triumph on her face. But there was more than triumph in the tone with which she answered Lupe.

"As long as we want to," she said.